At last.

Surely Aleck had waited days for this moment, not mere hours. Gently, gently… learning the shape of Tansy's mouth, the perfect bow, the lush fullness…wanting…more. Dizzy. Breathless. *Alive.*

Cupping her face in both hands, he shifted the angle, took the kiss deeper, tasted eagerness on her tongue. Sparks…heat…longing…

She fisted her hands in his t-shirt. Moaned. Rose on tiptoe, clutched the back of his head.

Ahhh. Holding her, winding himself around her warmth, gathering her in…breathing her in…aching…

Gasping, she spun away.

He stared at her through a red haze, chest heaving, gulping for air. "Tansy…" A tortured plea wrapped in her name.

She pressed a hand to her chest and swallowed. "I…have to…stop."

He closed his eyes and dragged in a breath. "Aye." Another breath, and another. Then he trusted himself to look at her. Even so, he took an involuntary step forward.

A COWBOY'S DESTINY

THE MCGAVIN BROTHERS

Vicki Lewis Thompson

Ocean Dance Press

Want more cowboys? Check out these other titles by Vicki Lewis Thompson

The McGavin Brothers
A Cowboy's Strength
A Cowboy's Honor
A Cowboy's Return
A Cowboy's Heart
A Cowboy's Courage
A Cowboy's Christmas
A Cowboy's Kiss
A Cowboy's Luck
A Cowboy's Charm
A Cowboy's Challenge
A Cowboy's Baby
A Cowboy's Holiday
A Cowboy's Choice
A Cowboy's Worth
A Cowboy's Destiny

Thunder Mountain Brotherhood
Midnight Thunder
Thunderstruck
Rolling Like Thunder
A Cowboy Under the Mistletoe
Cowboy All Night
Cowboy After Dark
Cowboy Untamed
Cowboy Unwrapped
In the Cowboy's Arms
Say Yes to the Cowboy
Do You Take This Cowboy?

Sons of Chance
Wanted!
Ambushed!
Claimed!
Should've Been a Cowboy
Cowboy Up
Cowboys Like Us
Long Road Home
Lead Me Home
Feels Like Home
I Cross My Heart
Wild at Heart
The Heart Won't Lie
Cowboys and Angels
Riding High
Riding Hard
Riding Home
A Last Chance Christmas

<u>**1**</u>

"Bloody hell, Rory, you don't need to buy me a Stetson." Aleck had been debating the point with his brother ever since leaving the airport in Bozeman. He'd been trained to argue effectively and was currently earning a living with that skill.

Despite that, he'd made no headway with Rory, who'd just pulled up in front of a clothing shop on Main Street. Like every other establishment in Eagles Nest, it was decorated with flags and bunting for the town's upcoming Independence Day celebration.

He glanced at his brother. "You are one bull-headed Scotsman."

Rory grinned as he turned off the motor of his pickup truck. "It's not like you'd be just findin' that out."

He sighed. "Nay."

"I'm tellin' you, it makes a difference. Everybody wears them around here. Clamp one on your head and you'll feel like you're a part of the community."

"But I'm not a part of the community. I'm goin' home in four days. Makes no sense for you to buy me a hat I'll never wear again."

"It'll shade your eyes. The sun's bright here."

"I have these." He gestured toward his sunglasses.

"They make you look like a city bloke."

"I am a city bloke. Why pretend I'm somethin' different?"

Rory shoved back his cowboy hat, which showed signs of wear and tear from daily use. "I'm not suggestin' that. But what's the harm in fallin' in with the local customs? And I can guarantee you'll enjoy the look and feel of a Stetson. It has gravitas."

"*Gravitas*?" Aleck laughed.

"Aye. Like the cowboys in those old movies we used to watch—John Wayne, Clint Eastwood, Steve McQueen."

"You watched 'em more than me."

"But you know what I'm talkin' about." He opened his door. "Besides, you'll need a Stetson when we walk into the Guzzlin' Grizzly for a pint. A hat is part of the GG dress code."

"Aye, right." He rolled his eyes.

"That might be stretchin' it a bit, but...come on in and try one. Won't kill you."

"I'll take a look, but if I decide to buy one, I'll pay for it, not you."

"We've been over this. Buyin' you this hat is my way of thankin' you for all you've done."

Aleck met his brother's gaze. Clearly this purchase was important to him. "All right." He opened his door and climbed out.

"You could also look at some boots while we're here." Rory crossed the sidewalk, opened the door, and held it for him.

"I don't think so." As he stepped inside, the scent of leather and pressed cotton stirred a memory, their ma taking them to buy school clothes. Hadn't shopped with his brother since then.

Rory turned left toward the men's section and a display of Western hats on the far wall. "I recommend you get a black one."

"Don't the bad guys wear those?" He tucked his sunglasses in his shirt pocket.

"Used to in the movies, but white is impractical for a working cowhand."

"Which I'm not." But his brother sure did look the part as he studied the choices, his thumbs hooked in the belt loops of his jeans. He'd taken to this life as if he'd been born to it.

He rocked back on the heels of his boots, which were polished, but creased from constant use. "Most everybody wears brown or black unless they go for a summer straw."

So far no sales clerk had come hurrying over, eager to help. Unusual. "It's summer, so maybe I should—"

"Not for your first hat."

"My *only* hat."

"You never know. You might fall in love with the way it looks and decide to get another in brown."

"I sincerely doubt it."

"You say that now." Rory plucked a black one off the display, holding it by the crown. "But wait until you see yourself in this beauty."

Aleck sighed, took the felt hat and settled it on his head. Saints alive, the thing fit perfectly. That never happened to him. He glanced at Rory, who was sporting his *I told you so* expression. "Lucky grab on your part."

"I might have come in here yesterday to check out the hats. We wear the same size."

Aleck examined the rough-hewn wall in front of them. A wee bit of green tape was stuck right below where this hat had hung. "Did you ask the sales staff to back off and leave this operation to you?"

His brother shrugged. "I know you better than they do."

"So what do you think?"

"See for yourself." Rory pointed out a full-length mirror in the back corner.

Aleck turned and started toward it. Then he paused, disconcerted by the image. Who was that bloke? Couldn't be him. Except the guy was wearing his shirt and jeans. He stared in the mirror. A cowboy stared back.

"Tug on the brim in front, bring it a wee bit lower."

He did as Rory suggested. Damned if it didn't make him look mysterious. He'd never looked mysterious in his life. He didn't now, either. His shoes took the mystery right out of the picture.

"If you're lookin' at those trainers and thinkin' you need to switch them out for boots, you would be right. Oh, and over here trainers are called runnin' shoes."

"Let me guess. Cowboys never wear 'em."

"Only if they're doin' somethin' that requires a lot of runnin'. Otherwise it's boots all the way."

"I see where this is headin'. The hat leads to boots which leads to..." He glanced at Rory. "I'm not cowboy material. If that's where you're goin' with this, then—"

"Didn't say you were, but since you're gettin' the hat, let me treat you to a nice pair of boots."

Aleck held up both hands. "No, I accepted the hat, but I'll pay for the boots."

"I'm gainfully employed brewin' beer and workin' for Aunt Kendra on the side. I can afford it." He sounded proud of the fact that he could do this for his big brother.

Which meant accepting his offer was the only choice. "Then thank you. Much appreciated. Once I put on the hat, I look like a numptie in these trainers."

"Exactly. Do you still wear the same size?"

"Yes, and I...did you preselect my boots, too?"

"Just in case you agreed to it. Didn't want to waste too much time here."

Twenty minutes later Aleck left the store, his boot heels hitting the wooden floor with authority. Boots announced his presence in a way trainers couldn't. They had...gravitas. He smiled. Rory might have a point, there.

"Watch you don't knock off your hat when you get in the truck."

"Probably better to take it off."

"Some do. I like wearin' mine. When I bought the truck, I made sure I had enough headroom for my hat."

Aleck took his off and climbed into the passenger seat. Then he put it back on. The crown didn't touch the headliner. "Evidently those old cowboy movies had quite an effect on you."

"Didn't realize how much until I arrived at Wild Creek Ranch. It looks like a movie set except it's real."

"Sounds like you're happy, then."

"Aye. More than I've ever been in my life. Not that I don't miss everybody. I do. I'll visit when I can manage it. I want Damaris to come with me."

"Ma and Da will love hearin' that. You obviously made the right choice, decidin' to live over here, but it's weird not havin' you around. I find myself pickin' up my phone to see if you want to go for a pint. Then I remember you're gone."

"I miss you, too." He pulled into the parking lot of a two-story, rustic saloon. "Like I said, I'll visit when I can."

"Let's hope it's soon." He glanced out the window. "So this is the famous Guzzlin' Grizzly?"

"This is it. The bar's been here forever, but it's been upgraded over the years. That said, nobody considered addin' a brewery until I came along. Luckily the property's big enough, so they pushed out the back wall and McGavin brewery became a reality."

"That's fast work, little brother."

Rory switched off the engine and turned to him. "It wasn't all my doin'. When the town throws its support behind a project, miracles happen. You've never seen anything like it."

"But you still had to produce those recipes practically overnight."

"After all those frustratin' months workin' in a bloody warehouse, I was ready. I was on fire to create somethin' special. I worked night and day."

"What about Damaris?"

"She was with me all the way. The woman's brilliant. It's not her field, but she caught on quick and we were a team. We'd work for hours, fall into bed, exhausted, and make love."

"She's truly your soul mate, then?"

"Aye. And I'm hers."

"I can't wait to meet her."

"She can't wait to meet you, either, but she thought I should come alone so we'd have time to catch up. Stoppin' at the GG is part of that. By the way, Michael's expectin' us."

"He's the bloke who co-owns this place with our cousin Bryce?"

"Aye."

"Does he know about your campaign to get me into a hat and boots?"

"I might have said somethin' to him."

"I see. More was ridin' on this than I thought." He was doubly glad he'd gone along with it. Rory would have lost face if he hadn't. "Anybody else in there in on it?"

"I said somethin' to Tansy."

"Who's that?"

"One of the bartenders. A good friend. Oh, and Jenny heard about it. She's our top server. Might remind you a wee bit of Ma. She told Ellen, who's second in command to Jenny."

"Why was everybody so interested?"

"Wagers were involved."

"Were they, now?"

"Folks around here enjoy a friendly wager now and then."

"I don't mind one, myself. Do you know which way folks bet?"

"Last I heard, Jenny and Ellen thought I'd succeed. Michael and Tansy went the other way. Tansy was the most vocal. She didn't think I had a snowball's chance in hell of talkin' you into it."

"Based on what? She doesn't know me."

"She knows you're a solicitor and she figured a lawyer wouldn't go for somethin' so illogical."

"Sound reasonin'. And for the record, it's not logical, but—"

"It vastly improves your look."

"Are you sayin' I have gravitas?"

"Aye." Rory nodded, his expression solemn except for the twinkle in his eyes. "That you do, laddie."

"Your head's full o' mince." Laughing, he climbed out of the truck. But as he crossed the parking lot beside his brother, he lengthened his stride, squared his shoulders and lifted his chin.

2

Although Monday afternoons were typically slow at the GG, all the flags and bunting around town must have put Eagles Nesters in a celebratory mood. Customers kept Tansy and Jenny hopping. As the only server on duty, Jenny scurried among the tables taking orders old school with paper and pen. The WiFi was down and the electronic order tablets were useless.

Despite hustling to fill orders, Tansy managed to keep an eye on the front door. Rory and his brother could arrive any minute. Money was on the line and the odds were in her favor.

Rory had admitted Aleck wasn't eager to take up riding and roping. He was here to see his brother and meet his relatives, not dive into the cowboy way of life. Besides, he'd be leaving in four days.

Therefore, she and Michael, co-owner of the GG, would split the pot. Jenny and Ellen, who'd made a sentimental bet that Rory would prevail stood to lose their ten bucks.

Or not. The front door opened and Rory sauntered in looking pleased as punch, followed by a broad-shouldered dude wearing a Stetson. And boots!

How could she have been so wrong? Either Rory was more persuasive than she'd given him credit for, or his brother had abandoned logic to please his little brother. She was going with option two, which gave Aleck McGavin a whole bunch of points in her book.

He looked damned good in the hat, too. Jenny hurried over to welcome him to the GG and he took it off, revealing wavy brown hair that hadn't had time to be imprinted by the hat.

He ran his fingers through it and said something that made Jenny laugh. The words were indistinct but the brogue came through. Tansy was a sucker for a good Scottish brogue.

Jenny escorted Aleck and Rory to the bar. "Our Scottish visitor prefers a bar stool to a table, Tansy, so he's all yours."

Fine with me. She gazed into smiling green eyes. "Welcome to Eagles Nest, Aleck."

"Thank you kindly, lass." He'd put his hat back on, likely because Rory or Jenny had said that was GG protocol.

"Love your accent."

"Love yours, too." He nudged back his hat and a lock of hair escaped, making him look rakish. "Boston, aye?"

"Good ear. What can I do for you?"

"Two pints of McGavin's pale ale, please. One for me and one for my brother."

The soft burr in his voice warmed her all over. "Anything else?"

"Not for me." He turned to Rory. "But if you want somethin' to eat..."

"No, thanks. I'm savin' up for the big family feast at the ranch tonight."

"Then I'll get your drafts." Tansy had looked forward to the moment when Aleck tasted Rory's signature brew. She picked up two logo mugs, filled them slowly with shimmering gold liquid and topped them off with a perfect head of ivory foam. Placing them gently on a GG coaster, she stepped back.

"Hey, now, those deserve a picture." Aleck pulled out his phone.

Jenny was headed over with more orders, but Tansy had a minute to spare. "Let me take one of the two of you."

"Even better." Aleck handed her the phone. "I'll send it to Ma and Da."

"Pick up the mugs like you're doing a toast."

"Good idea."

She snapped a picture as both men lifted their beer.

Aleck started to take a drink and paused. "I should do a proper toast. This is historic." He raised his mug in Rory's direction.

"Hang on a sec." Tansy looked back at Jenny standing beside the bar. "Be right with you. I need to video this."

Jenny nodded. "Go for it."

"Okay, Aleck. You're on." She tapped the button.

He sent her a quick smile and faced Rory. "To my talented brother and the noble brew he created, one that proudly bears the McGavin name. *Slainte Mhor.*"

Rory grinned. "You haven't even tasted it, yet. Could be mingin'."

"Not if you made it." He took a sip. "Ahhh. Nectar of the gods."

Tansy hit the stop button. "Perfect." She returned the phone.

"Thanks, lass."

"You're most welcome." She took the orders from Jenny, grabbed glasses and began mixing drinks.

"Sending it to Ma and Da now. It's ten there, so they might be in bed, but likely not yet. They'll want to see this."

"And send it to me," Rory said. "I want a copy."

Tansy set the drinks on Jenny's tray. "Any chance I can get a copy?"

"Aye, but I don't have your—"

"I have it," Rory said. "Give me your phone and I'll send it to me and to her."

Tansy smiled. That had worked out nicely. Didn't hurt to exchange digits, even if he was only here for a few days.

Orders came in thick and fast after that and she didn't have another chance to talk to either of the brothers. Judging from their animated conversation, they'd enjoyed a quick response from their folks after sending the video. Some teasing must have been going on, because both men did a lot of laughing as they drank their ale.

"Hey, guys," she called down to them when they'd almost finished. "Want another?"

"Better not," Rory said. "Aunt Kendra texted to ask if we'd be showin' up soon so we—"

"There he is!" Michael came out of the office wearing the men's version of the black logo t-shirt Tansy had on. In the tight shirt he looked more like a bouncer than the GG's co-owner. He crossed to the bar and shook hands with Aleck. "Welcome to the GG. Jenny told me you were here, but I was on a very frustrating call with our internet provider."

Tansy glanced at her boss. "It's finally fixed, I hope. Jenny and I have been flying on one wing."

"I think we're good. Jenny just reported that the order tablets are working again. Let me know if you still have issues upstairs."

"Thanks. I'll check when my shift's over."

"You have WiFi tablets for the servers?" Aleck seemed impressed.

"We do," Michael said. "Old West ambiance paired with the latest technology."

"And I'm grateful," Tansy said. "It makes the restaurant and bar more efficient and I have WiFi in my apartment. Didn't realize how much I relied on that until it went down last night."

"It should be okay, now."

Aleck glanced at Michael's shirt. "That Guzzlin' Grizzly logo is amazin'."

"It's my wife Roxanne's creation. We're slapping it on everything. Folks love it."

"It's brilliant. Do you sell the shirts?"

"Yep. In the GG Country Store."

"I'll buy one on the way out."

"Too late," Rory said. "Yours is at the ranch waitin' for you."

"Hey, you already bought me—"

"The shirt's from the GG," Michael said. "We give 'em out to all visiting Scots."

"Better be careful with that kind of offer. My whole family's liable to descend on you one of these days."

"I hope they do. We have plenty of shirts. We stock other colors, but your brother seemed to think you needed a black one."

"To go with your black hat," Rory said.

Tansy smiled. "That'll make two green-eyed guys in black hats and black logo shirts walking around town. Do you suppose people will get you mixed up?"

Michael shook his head. "Not once they hear Aleck's brogue. Surprised the heck out of me that you'd agree to wear them, though."

"Same here," Tansy said.

Aleck glanced her way. "Guess I'm responsible for you losin' a bet. Sorry."

"Rory told you?"

"I didn't say anything until afterward," Rory said. "I had enough trouble convincin' him. He didn't need to know folks were bettin' ten bucks on it."

"Your prediction was logical." Aleck rested his forearms on the bar. "It's just that other factors came into play."

"I figured that out." She could listen to him all day long. The way he pronounced *just* as *joost* tickled her. "No worries. I only bet what I can afford to lose."

His warm gaze met hers. "Me, too."

Mm, nice. How many days would he be here? The computer screen behind the bar lit up with drink orders relayed from Jenny's tablet and she was forced to break eye contact. "Excuse me. Gotta get back to work. It was great meeting you, Aleck."

"It was my pleasure, lass." His words were lovely, but the gleam in his eyes had been even better. He stood.

"We'll be off, then." Rory got up, too. "We may be back tonight, although—"

"I hope you can make it," Michael said. "Bryce and Nicole's new show is terrific. I watched them rehearse yesterday and they blew me away."

Aleck might come back tonight? Tansy pretended she wasn't eavesdropping as she continued mixing drinks.

"I'd like to plan on it." Aleck sounded enthusiastic. "Rory sent me an album and I'm determined to catch their show at least once while I'm here." He turned to his brother. "Could we do that after dinner tonight?"

"We could, but you just took a long trip. I thought you might want to have an early—"

"Nay. I can sleep when I get back to Scotland. I'll only be here a few days. I'd like to see that performance tonight in case other things come up that would keep me from going later in the week."

"Alrighty. Damaris will probably want to, then, and the rest of the family might drive in for it if you're goin'."

"That would be great. Oh, and Tansy, can I ask you somethin'?"

"What's that?" She'd snapped to attention a bit too fast. *Cool it, girl.*

"Did I hear you say that you live upstairs?"

"Yes, I do."

"Would you be willin' to join us tonight?"

"Of course. I was tentatively planning to come down for the show. Now I'll be sure to." Yeah, eagerness was sticking out all over her. Couldn't be helped.

"I'll text you when we're headin' into town."

"Okay." She answered his smile with one of her own. "I'll see you then."

"Lookin' forward to it. Nice meetin' you, Michael." He followed Rory out the door.

Michael pushed away from the bar and glanced at her. "Guess we're both ten bucks poorer."

"I don't care. I'm positive he did it for Rory's sake, because he could tell Rory was set on it. That's sweet."

"Yeah, it's obvious they're close. The rest of the family must be special, too, judging from the way Rory talks about them. Makes it even more amazing that he decided to live so far away from his entire family."

"I don't think he had a choice once he met Damaris. He might have said he didn't move here because of her. He might even believe it. But she was the real reason he left Scotland."

"You're probably right. In any case, he's obviously happy with that decision. But I'll bet he misses his family, especially Aleck."

"Well, sure."

"Do you think the hat and boots campaign could be the first step in trying to lure Aleck into moving here?"

"If it is, he's doomed to fail. His brother's a lawyer with an established practice in Scotland. That's a skill that doesn't translate to a different country."

"Do you know that for a fact?"

"I come from a family of Harvard lawyers. Trust me, it's tough enough to transfer from one state to another. Heading to a different country means essentially starting over."

"Well, yeah, you'd have to build a new client list, but—"

"It's way more than that. You have to earn a degree from an accredited school in the US before you can even take the bar exam."

"No kidding?"

"That's how it works."

"Huh. Too bad. Well, it's back to work for me."

"Same here. Thanks for persevering with the WiFi."

"You bet." He headed to his office.

Grabbing a bar rag, she walked over to where Aleck and Rory had been sitting. The edge of a bill protruded from under Aleck's empty mug.

She picked up the mug and smiled. Seemed she wasn't ten bucks poorer, after all.

<u>3</u>

"That pale ale is outstandin'." Aleck tugged the brim of his new hat a wee bit lower to shade his eyes as he fell into step beside Rory. "I'm glad we're comin' back tonight so I can have another pint."

Rory chuckled. "Is that the only reason you're glad we're comin' back?"

"What do you think?"

"I think I'm surprised."

"Why?"

"She's got pink hair."

"Just a few streaks. It's mostly blonde."

"There's some purple in there, too."

"So what?"

"I've never known you to fancy a lass who dyes her hair unnatural colors."

"I've got nothin' against it. Ladies in my profession don't have rainbow-colored hair. That's the pool I've been drawin' from." Her hair had made him smile. Then he'd gazed into those big brown eyes. He'd never had such a visceral reaction to any lass.

"You only have four days." Rory dug his keys out of his jeans pocket as they approached the truck. "Less than that, really."

"Aye. Not much time, is it?"

Rory paused next to the tailgate and gazed at him. "There's a solution. Go back to your original plan and stay through the weekend."

"That wouldn't go over well with Campbell. He told everyone to be at that meetin' or else."

"He'd fire you over missin' a meetin'?"

"Wouldn't put it past him, especially if we end up losin' this client. He'll want a scapegoat."

"That's well radge."

"Aye, but I'm not riskin' my livelihood."

"You've got yourself a wee window, then." Rory headed toward the driver's side.

"Yep, I do." He walked to the other side and climbed into the passenger seat. "I plan to make the most of it."

"The hat will help."

He gave his brother a long look.

"Well, it will." As he put the truck in reverse and started to back out, his phone chimed. "That's Damaris." Putting on the brakes, he changed gears and pulled the truck back into the space. Then he tapped the screen and answered the call on speaker mode. "Hey, there. Aleck and I are leavin' the GG now. We should be—"

"Mandy's in labor."

"For real this time?"

"Oh, it's real, all right. We were all sitting on the porch when her water broke."

"So now what—"

"Zane decided not to drive her home. That road's too bumpy. Instead he carried her back to Kendra's bedroom and called the midwife, who should be arriving any minute. Kendra and April, who know more about this than any of us, say she'll probably have that kid within the next hour or so."

"Jesus, Joseph and Mary."

"I thought I should warn you. It's crazy around here. Not quite the relaxed welcome we'd planned for Aleck."

Aleck leaned closer to the phone. "Don't worry about me, lass. I'll be fine." It was the right response, even though he'd never attended a birthing, not even as a bystander in a hospital waiting room. A home delivery sounded more intense. If he had a choice, he'd—

"Hey, Aleck! Good to hear your voice. Can't wait to meet you."

"I'm eager to meet you, too. Thanks for lettin' us know about the bairn."

"We're on our way." Rory checked his rearview mirror and backed out of the parking space. "Anythin' you need from town, lass?"

"I don't think so. The supplies are all at Zane and Mandy's house. Jo and Brendan have gone over to get them. The midwife's on her way."

"We'll be there as soon as we can." Rory headed for the parking lot exit.

"See you then. Love you."

"Love you, too." He disconnected the call and glanced at Aleck before pulling into traffic. "Excitin', huh?"

"Sure is. Did you tell me this might happen? Because if you did, I can't—"

"Didn't bother tellin' you." He pulled out on the two-lane road heading out of town. "She isn't due until Fourth of July, and Aunt Kendra said first bairns are usually late. I didn't want you to get your hopes up because I figured you'd probably miss seein' it."

He sucked in a breath. "Are we expected to watch?"

"Would you like to?"

"Good God, no. I'm still traumatized from the film they showed us in school."

Rory chuckled. "Dinna fash yourself, then. Wouldn't be room for you in there, anyway. I count five who'll have ringside seats—Zane, Jo, Kendra, April and the midwife."

"Jo is Mandy's mother?"

"Aye."

"Who's Brendan?"

"Brendan Sawyer, Jo's new husband and Quinn's brother. Their wedding was a couple weeks ago, so Damaris might not have updated the spreadsheet I sent to you. Have you had a chance to study it?"

"On the plane. Guess I could use this time to look at it again." He pulled out his phone and began scrolling through the McGavin/Sawyer cheat sheet with a bonus section on anyone remotely connected to either of the families. After several minutes, he glanced over at Rory. "It'll be like keeping the characters straight in *War and Peace*."

"At least you got her spreadsheet in advance. Don't know what I would've done if she hadn't shared it with me on my first day."

"I'm grateful to have it." He put away his phone. "And I'll do my best, but I hope they're a forgivin' bunch."

"They are."

"I'll do better once I'm face-to-face with 'em. For now it's just a long list of folks."

"You'll only have the McGavin bunch to deal with at first, plus Quinn, Brendan and Jo."

"That'll be plenty, although I feel like I already know Bryce and Nicole from listenin' to their music and seeing their picture on the album cover."

"Speakin' of pictures, didn't I send you some from Ryker and April's weddin'? That should help."

"Aye. Ryker and April will be easy to spot. You said April will go into the room with Mandy, though. Why's that?"

"She's a massage therapist and massage can help a woman through labor, or so I'm told. Mandy was countin' on her bein' there. In a way, this comes at a good time. All the important people are already gathered."

"Did they plan to have a home birth, or is it just workin' out that way?"

"That's what they wanted. They're prepared for it at their house, which is why Jo and Brendan had to drive over there and fetch everythin'."

"Sounds like everyone knows what they're doin', then. That makes me feel better."

"Faith and Cody do, for sure. Faith had Noel at home right before Christmas. She and Cody live in an A-frame a short hike from the main house and Noel was born there. Come to think of it, Mandy might want Faith in with her, too, since she just went through this. It'll be a full room."

"Then if I spot a guy holdin' a six-month-old bairn, that'll be Cody with Noel."

"Likely, unless somebody else has her. She's popular with this bunch. Gets passed around a lot." He put on his signal and made a right onto a dirt road marked by a wooden sign for Wild Creek Ranch.

"And she's okay with bein' passed around?"

"She loves it. That wee lass is pure tidy."

Aleck laughed. "Never thought I'd hear you ravin' about a bairn. Next thing I know, you'll want one of your own."

"Damaris and I have already talked about it."

"After only knowin' her for two months?"

"Two and a half. That's enough. Besides, it's just talk for now. We're pickin' names and such."

Aleck scrambled for purchase on this unfamiliar territory. "I thought this was a wee cabin you're rentin'. Barely enough room to turn around."

"A bairn won't take up much room."

"But they grow."

"We'll have a bigger place by then. We've checked with Aunt Kendra about buyin' a small plot of ranch land. She's excited about that."

"Does this procreatin' plan include a weddin'?"

"Aye."

"Good, because Ma will want that. Da, too, for that matter."

"We're waitin' until Damaris publishes her research paper. Then we'll tie the knot and start multiplyin'. Another year or two and you'll be an uncle, for sure."

"That's soberin'."

"That's life, big brother. I'm in the full flood of it now that I'm with Damaris. At Wild Creek Ranch, you feel the current movin' around you. Makes you eager to dive in and be part of it."

"I can see that. You're a whirlin' dervish."

"My energy is focused, though. I know what I want and how to get it."

"Not many can say that."

"You always could." He shifted to a lower gear. "Get ready for your first glimpse of the ranch. It's right around this bend. And it's just like you'd expect a ranch to look."

"Not sure I have an image in my head of the perfect ranch."

"You will in a few seconds." Rory navigated the turn and the ranch buildings came into view. "There it is." He made the announcement with pride and affection. "Wild Creek Ranch."

Aleck drew in a breath. "It's somethin', all right. I can see why it appeals to you." But he was completely out of his element. His experience with rural life was confined to his grandparents' sheep farm, which was a wee operation compared to this extensive layout.

Maybe it was the rugged, snow-tipped mountains that gave the ranch more heft, like an imposing frame surrounding a painting. A thick pine forest circled the clearing where the buildings stood.

To his right were two large barns, one old and majestic, the other more modern. Both looked freshly painted. A sturdy paddock, what they probably called a corral over here, was currently empty, but a sizeable herd of horses grazed in a green pasture so vast that he couldn't see where the boundary fence ended.

Then there was the impressive main house. Several pickup trucks in various colors were parked in an area to the right of it, and what looked like an outdoor eating area with picnic tables took up a fair amount of space on the left. Could seat more than a hundred people at those tables, easy.

A front porch ran the length of the house with a dozen wooden rockers spaced every couple of feet. No one was on the porch, though. He cleared his throat. "Never saw a house made of logs except in the movies."

"I love that about it." Rory drove toward the line of trucks. "Wait'll you get inside. The big stone fireplace is somethin'. It won't be goin' now, but if we get that rain that's predicted, they might stoke it up later."

"Where's your cabin?"

"Up that hill to the right, past the parking area. It's hidden in the trees, which is nice because....ah, there's Damaris. Must've been watchin' for us."

A bonnie dark-haired woman in jeans and a bright yellow t-shirt hurried down the front porch steps. She pushed her glasses against the bridge of her nose and gave them a wave.

Rory tapped the horn and pulled in next to the last truck in the row. Shutting off the engine, he climbed out and called to Damaris. "Has Mandy had—"

"Not yet! Might be another hour or so."

It wasn't the news Aleck had hoped for. Birthing a babe had looked painful in the one and only video he'd seen. He would've been happy for that part to be over and done with. Quite likely Mandy wished the same. He rounded the truck as Damaris gave Rory a hug and a quick kiss.

Then she turned to him with a brilliant smile. "Hey, Aleck!" Closing the distance between them, she gave him an enthusiastic hug that almost knocked off his hat and left her glasses sitting crooked on her nose. She straightened them. "You look just like your pictures! I'm so glad you're here."

"Me, too, lass. Me, too." Such a happy face. "You look just like your pictures, too."

"That's good to hear. Not everyone does, you know."

"They don't?"

"Point a camera at some people and they freeze up, which makes them seem all stern and forbidding when they're not like that at all. But you projected friendliness in your pictures and you do the same in person, too."

"Oh, he can project stern and forbiddin'," Rory said. "You should see his courtroom face."

"Clearly you don't have your courtroom face on now."

"Nay, this is my overwhelmed and jetlagged face."

She peered at him. "I understand jetlagged, but why overwhelmed?"

"All this." He spread his arms. "The barns, the horses, the huge mountains, a house built with giant felled trees. Rory described the ranch to me, but I didn't grasp the scale."

"I guess it could be daunting if you've never been here. I grew up in Eagles Nest and came out to Wild Creek all the time, so to me it seems cozy."

"I wouldn't have used that word."

She grinned. "Give yourself time. It'll grow on you. By the way, the hat is perfect. And the boots." She glanced at Rory. "Well done, you."

"He made me work for it." Rory flashed his brother a grin. "Down to the wire, it was. But the minute he put on the hat, I had him."

"My *preselected* hat. It was a setup."

"But aren't you glad you caved?" Damaris gave him an approving once-over. "The hat suits you."

"For the time bein', anyway."

"I'll bet you liked having it on when you walked into the GG."

"Aye. I can admit that much." Mainly because Tansy had seemed to enjoy the fact that he was wearing it.

"How'd you like the pale ale?"

"Best I've ever tasted."

"Wow, really? After all the wonderful brews in your part of the world?"

"Really. You and Rory did a bang-up job. I'm takin' a few bottles back with me."

"Excellent! Well, we'd better unload your stuff and get you inside. Did your bagpipes make it through security?"

"Aye."

"Then we can finalize your parade entry with Ellie Mae. I didn't want to do that until you arrived with them, so you're just listed as *McGavin entry, TBD.*"

"The security folks asked me to play 'em to prove the pipes weren't a bomb in disguise, but when I said I would, they let me go through without doin' it."

"Just so you know," Rory said, "I've been practicin' faithfully, drummin' my heart out on the front porch of our cabin."

"Did you rent a drum?"

"Bought it. Felt good to get those sticks in my hand again. I've missed playin', especially with you."

"I've missed havin' you there, too. Some of us had a gig down to Paisley a couple of weeks ago for their car show. Felt strange goin' without you."

"Hey, guys," Damaris said. "I just had the most awesome idea. What if Rory fetches his drum from the cabin? Then after the baby's born, you two can give baby McGavin a proper Scottish welcome."

Eyebrows raised, Aleck looked over at Rory. "In the house would be too loud, but maybe on the porch."

Rory smiled. "You know what they say—the pipes and drum make everything better."

"It's the God's truth. And I know just the tune we'll play. Let's get movin'. That bairn could show up anytime now."

"You take the pipes." Rory reached behind the luggage net in the truck bed. "I'll get your suitcase."

"Hold on," Damaris said. "I see dust. Someone's coming."

Rory turned toward the road. "Huh. That's Tansy's wee purple truck."

A pleasant jolt of adrenaline hit as Aleck followed his gaze. "Why would she be here?"

"I don't...oh, wait. I know exactly why." Rory looked at Damaris. "McGavin's Baby Brew."

"*McGavin's Baby Brew*?" Aleck stared at them. "What's wrong with you? You can't give alcohol to a brand new bairn!"

Damaris smiled at him. "Why not?"

"Because...because...I don't know! It just seems like a terrible idea!"

"She's teasin' you, big brother. We call it McGavin's Baby Brew because we created it to honor the birth. We won't be givin' it to the wee one. Just the adults."

"Oh."

"And we forgot all about it," Damaris said.

"Sure did." Rory shook his head. "I can see myself rememberin' about the time everybody's ready to toast the bairn. Evidently word got to the

GG." He turned to Aleck. "We need to move that ale into Aunt Kendra's pantry fridge and I'd like to sneak it in if we can."

"Nobody in there knows you made this?"

"Nay. It's a secret recipe. The only ones who've tasted it are Damaris, me, Tansy and Michael. Even Bryce doesn't know what we've been up to. Roxanne does, because she created the label, but she's a vault."

"Keepin' it a secret must have taken some doin'."

"Oh, it did. I hope nobody saw Tansy's truck." He waved to her and pointed toward the side of the house. "C'mon." He started in that direction. "We need to get out of sight so we can hatch a plan."

No kidding. As he followed Rory and Damaris, he took several deep breaths. Tansy's unexpected arrival had stirred him up in a good way. He was very glad she was here.

4

When Michael had offered to take the cases of McGavin's Baby Brew out to the ranch, Tansy had convinced him she should do it since she was nearing the end of her shift. If delivering the beer gave her another chance to see Aleck, so much the better.

Considering her reaction to him earlier, she could use a reality check. A second encounter might reveal that he wasn't as incredibly gorgeous and charming as he'd seemed. After driving around to the side of the house, she rolled down the window as Rory arrived, followed by Damaris and...Aleck. Still gorgeous.

"Tansy, thank the Lord." Rory leaned an arm on the roof of the truck and ducked his head so he could talk with her. "Damaris and I totally forgot."

"No worries. Has that baby made an appearance, yet?"

"Nope." Damaris slid an arm around Rory's waist. "Could be another half hour or so."

"Then this beer won't be anticlimactic." She smiled at Aleck, who'd moved in on Damaris's other side. "Hi, there."

"Good to see you again, lass."

"Same here." She pushed her sunglasses to the top of her head. Meeting his gaze produced goosebumps, so evidently she remained highly susceptible to his Scottish charm. She turned back to Rory. "What's the plan?"

"If you drive around to the back door, we might be able to smuggle it into the pantry without anybody noticing. Maybe."

"You'd have a better chance with a diversion," Aleck said.

"Like what?" Staring at him certainly created one for her.

"Damaris and I could go in the front door with my suitcase and pipes while you and Rory drive around back and unload the ale."

"Pipes? As in bagpipes?"

"Aye. Brought 'em for the parade."

"Cool." A lawyer dude who played the bagpipes. He became more interesting by the minute. "But if you and Damaris go in without Rory, won't they ask where he is?"

"I'll just say he's up at the cabin fetchin' his drum for the big event."

"That works." Tansy put the truck in gear. "Hop in, Rory."

"Okay, but what'll you do when we're finished unloadin' the baby brew?"

"Hope that I can make a clean getaway."

"That *seems* unfair," Damaris said. "Don't you want to stay until that cutie-pie's born?"

"Well, sure, but I can't just show up for no reason. I'm not family, so—"

Aleck pulled out his phone. "Take this." He handed it to her. "You can say I left it at the Guzzlin' Grizzly and you're returnin' it."

"Brilliant." Damaris nodded in approval. "They'll insist you stay after taking the trouble to drive out here."

"Good plan. Let's move out." Rory started around the truck.

"See you two in a bit." Aleck tipped his hat and walked away with Damaris.

Tansy put the truck in gear. "Did you teach him to tip his hat?"

"Why, did he just do it?"

"Like a pro." She drove slowly around the house, following a faint track through dirt and clumps of wild grass.

Rory chuckled. "He's gettin' into this. I can tell he loves the hat."

"Are you going to get him on a horse while he's here?" She braked for a squirrel.

"Hope so. We'll see how it goes. By the way, he wants to see Bryce and Nicole's show. Are they still playin' tonight?"

"They told Michael they will if the baby comes as fast as everyone's predicting."

"Aleck's a little nervous about the home birth idea, but personally, I'm glad he arrived durin' a big family moment."

Tansy smiled. "Just like you did."

"I know. Couldn't plan it better if I'd tried." He leaned forward as they rounded the side of the house. "If you swing out and back up to the stoop, we can unload easier."

"Okay." She maneuvered her sassy little pickup into position. She'd arrived in Eagles Nest in a nondescript sedan. Now she had *this*.

Rory hopped out. "Let me see if the coast is clear." In a few moments, he was back. "Everybody's makin' a fuss over Aleck and his bagpipes. We have great cover."

"Excellent." She got out and let down the tailgate.

"I'll take 'em in. Just stand in the back and feed me the cases."

"Got it." She vaulted to the bed of the truck. Working quickly, she'd soon handed over the entire stash. As Rory took the last case, the wail of a bagpipe drifted from the front of the house.

Her pulse jumped. "He's playing for them?"

"Aye." Rory grinned. "Likely standin' on the porch. The Great Highland pipes have too much volume for a livin' room concert."

"I was looking forward to the parade before, and now I really am. Your brother's a fascinating man, Rory."

He gazed at her. "Probably shouldn't tell you this, but he thinks you're fascinatin', too."

"Thanks." The info sent a conga line dancing through her midsection. "Good to know."

"Just wanted to give you a heads-up." He leaped down from the stoop and closed the tailgate. "We're done. The pantry fridge is stocked with McGavin's Baby Brew."

"Then let's join the party." After they climbed into the cab, she drove around the house.

Every note of the bagpipe tickled her nerve endings. She stopped the truck before leaving the shadow cast by the house. "Can you see if anyone's on the front porch besides Aleck?"

"Just him and he's..." Rory started to laugh. "He's positioned himself so he's blocking the door."

"Clever."

"I'll get out here and hotfoot it up to the cabin to fetch my snare drum."

"I didn't realize you're a drummer."

"For years. Used to play in a pipe band with Aleck. Gave mine away when I left Scotland, so I had to buy one for the parade. We've decided to play a tribute to the bairn when he or she arrives."

"What fun! And thanks for letting me stay."

"It's only fittin'." He opened his door and climbed down. "You were our chief consultant on the baby brew. You deserve to be here when everyone tastes it and raves."

"Thanks, Rory. I loved helping." And it was paying more benefits than she could have imagined. A bagpipe serenade. And a Scotsman who found her fascinating.

5

Damaris had been a key component in creating the perfect diversion. The minute he'd unpacked the pipes, she'd begged him to play *The Skye Boat Song* from *Outlander*. He should have expected it after Rory had told him she was a fan. While several people had urged him to perform in the living room, he'd talked them out of it.

By moving to the porch, he'd save their eardrums and block the door so nobody would be able to wander outside looking for Rory. Too bad his brother wasn't there to see Damaris's blissful reaction to hearing the tune live on the Great Highland pipes.

When he finished and the applause died down, someone asked for *Amazing Grace*. He'd played it so many times he didn't have to think at all. Instead he put everything he had into entrancing his clan so they wouldn't notice the beer transfer taking place in the pantry.

His clan. He'd brought the pipes so he and Rory could march together in the parade, but surely this performance was more significant. For the town folk, the pipes would be entertainment.

For his cousins, sons of Uncle Ian, nephews of his Da and Ma, they were a message from home.

Toward the end of *Amazing Grace*, Rory showed up with his snare drum. Without pausing between numbers, Aleck moved smoothly from the hymn to *Scotland the Brave*. The lively marching tune needed a drum beat to give it extra snap and Rory had a gift for that instrument.

Aleck's chest tightened a wee bit. He'd missed playing music with his brother. Their pipe band had been most active in their early twenties but it was still going. Just not with Rory in it.

About halfway through *Scotland the Brave,* Aunt Kendra came tearing down the hall waving her arms in the air. "The baby's coming! The baby's coming!" Then she raced back to the bedroom.

During the excited chatter that followed, Aleck glanced at Rory. "Are you still up for playin' a tribute to the bairn when we get the all-clear signal?"

"If you are."

"Try and stop me. I'm in performance mode now."

Rory grinned. "I keep forgettin' you're a showoff."

"Oh, like you're not. I seem to remember—"

"Are you guys going inside?"

He turned and gazed into brown eyes sparkling with amusement, as if she knew he was a yellow-bellied coward. "Fancy meetin' you here, lass."

"I know, right? What a coinkidink." She whisked through the door.

He waited until Rory went in before he picked up his hat and followed. The sight of Tansy was doing crazy things to his breathing and he needed to handle that. Inside, everyone was milling around and, if he wasn't mistaken, placing bets on the sex of the bairn.

Muffled groans from the back of the house told him the birthing was still in progress. Putting his fingers in his ears wouldn't be dignified. Heading back to the porch would mark him as spineless.

He found the spot near the door where Rory had left his drum and laid his pipes next to it. What to do with his hat? At last he spotted a coat tree where others had left theirs and found an empty hook.

"Here's your phone."

He turned and Tansy was right behind him. Bless her timing. She'd shifted his focus away from the birthing room.

No obstacles separated them—not an antique wooden bar or the door of her purple truck. He was close enough to touch her. He wanted to, but had no excuse. Her black t-shirt was lint-free.

She handed over the phone without so much as a brush of her fingers, but she leaned in and lowered her voice. "The forgotten phone was a clever idea, by the way."

"Thanks." He inhaled a sweet scent, maybe perfume or shampoo. "Should I make a big deal out of you returnin' it? Or have you told—"

"I mentioned it to Bryce and Nicole. That should be enough. Like Damaris predicted, they urged me to stick around. They seemed happy that I had an excuse to drive out."

"So am I."

"Me, too."

In this light, her eyes didn't look quite so brown. Bits of gold were mixed in. No wonder they sparkled. A light dusting of freckles across her nose gave her—

"And I get to hear you play the bagpipes. I've always liked them. I—"

"The baby's here!" Aunt Kendra's announcement touched off a hearty cheer.

"Boy or girl?" someone called out.

"Boy!"

"How's Mandy?" asked someone else.

"She's good." Aunt Kendra's voice was choked with happy tears as Quinn put a supporting arm around her waist. "Handled it like a champ, but Zane's a wreck."

A ripple of sympathetic laughter greeted that news.

"Hey, Mom," Bryce said, "when do we get to see the little guy?"

"Soon. He's getting cleaned up. He's—"

"He's absolutely beautiful!" A woman with her hair in a long braid walked up beside Kendra.

"He sure is!" April came down the hall and joined them. "Zane just promised me that once he pulls himself together, he'll bring that little guy out for a brief photo op."

"Does he have a name?" asked another cowboy who looked like a McGavin. "I'm not asking for myself," the guy continued as he hoisted a wee bairn to his shoulder. "Noel wants to know what to call her new cousin."

"No name, yet," Aunt Kendra said. "He showed up before Mandy and Zane had made a final decision. I'm sure he'll have one soon." She glanced around the room. "I wasn't prepared for this, either. I don't have bubbly chilling. We'll have to use whatever beverages we have on hand to toast Baby McGavin."

Rory stepped forward. "Aunt Kendra, The GG Brewery has you covered."

"It does?"

"Aye." He looked over at Damaris and Tansy. "Want to help me bring in the celebratory beverage?"

"You bet." Damaris headed toward the kitchen.

"Wait." Kendra held up her hand. "Is there something in my kitchen I don't know about?"

"Now there is," Rory said. "Thanks to my brother distractin' everybody with his bagpipe serenade."

"That was a diversion?"

"Aye."

"I see." She took a shaky breath. "It sounds like a first-rate surprise and I'd hate for anyone to miss it. I'll find out if Zane's recovered from—"

"I'm here, Mom." Zane came down the hall cradling an impossibly tiny bundle in his arms. "And Mandy wants to join us, too. Aunt Jo thinks that if—"

"Ryker! Trevor!" A slender woman with short gray hair stood in the hallway. "Mandy needs that four-handed chair maneuver you boys do. If you would be so kind."

"Of course." Ryker started toward her and Trevor followed.

"Well, then." Kendra smiled. "Looks like everyone will be here shortly. Let's wait for them, okay, Rory?"

"Absolutely. We'll go ahead and set up, and you give us the word."

Tansy smiled at Aleck. "Be right back."

"If everyone else will stay put," Zane said, "I'll make a circuit of the room so you all have a chance to see him."

Nicole held up her phone. "Can we take pictures?"

"Yes, but no flash, please."

"Wouldn't dream of it."

Aleck admired Zane's protective stance. Every newborn should be blessed with parents who possessed those instincts.

He'd expected the American McGavins to be good people because Rory had said so. But Aleck had promised his ma he'd make an independent evaluation. Less than an hour of fraternizing with the McGavins and he agreed with Rory. Ma and Da could relax.

Zane made his way around the room, which inevitably brought him to Aleck. "Welcome. Glad you could be here for this."

"Thank you. It's been an amazin' day. I've never seen a newborn before." He stared at the blotchy, wrinkled little face, more like that of a wizened old man than a just-arrived human. But an old man wouldn't have a head of dark hair sticking out in all directions. "He's...he's..."

"Incredible?"

"Aye. That he is. That's the word for him, all right. Incredible." He looked at Zane to gauge whether that lame delivery would pass muster.

Amusement flashed in his cousin's eyes. "It's okay, Aleck. I was in the same fix when Noel was born. She was all red and wrinkly, too. I'll tell you what Quinn told me. Just say *now that's a baby* and you're off the hook."

Aleck smiled. "I'll remember for next time. I'm happy for you, though. Can't imagine what it's like, being a father."

"It's scary as hell." He shifted the bundle in his arms. "I'd better keep going or I won't make it around the room in this century. We'll talk later. Loved the bagpipe serenade, what I heard of it." He moved on to Bryce and Nicole.

Nicole knew her lines. She raved about the bairn and called him *sweet, precious* and *adorable* as she took several pictures.

Ryker and Trevor arrived with Mandy perched on the seat they'd created with their forearms. They gently lowered her to a chair Quinn brought over. Zane finished his rounds and Kendra signaled to Rory.

He ducked into the kitchen. Shortly after that, he, Damaris and Tandy came out, each of them carrying a serving tray loaded with bottles of beer.

Holding his tray aloft, Rory cleared his throat. "I feel like shoutin' this out, but that wouldn't be good for the wee one, so I'll tone it down. May I present a GG limited edition, McGavin's Baby Brew."

"Aww!" Kendra pressed her hand to her heart.

"Brewed by Damaris and me," Rory continued, "taste tested by Tansy and Michael, label designed by Roxanne. Enjoy."

All three servers wound their way through the crowd in a seemingly random pattern, but Tansy managed to finish up next to Aleck with two bottles left on her tray. He grabbed both and she slid the tray onto a nearby end table.

He handed one to her. The label featured a bairn dressed in pink Western wear on one side and the same image in blue on the opposite side.

Ryker held his beer aloft. "Mom? You get first dibs on the toast."

She swiped at her eyes and gulped. "I'm a hot mess, son. You'd better do it."

His expression softened. "Sure thing." He faced his brother and sister-in-law. "To Mandy and Zane, who've blessed us with another member of the clan. And to Baby McGavin, who was so eager to be here that he rushed the gate. We're all very—" He paused and looked at Mandy. "You're not going to drink that for real, are you?"

"Just taking a teensy sip for now. But in the next several weeks, I'll be drinking beer. It's good for milk production, so I'm particularly excited about this signature brew."

"Okay, then. Just a sip, though."

She gave him a sweet smile. "You're not the boss of me, Ryker McGavin."

Zane grinned at his brother. "Just like old times."

Ryker rolled his eyes. "As I was saying, here's to Mandy, Zane, and their newborn child. May they always—"

"I sure wish we had a name to go with this toast," Trevor said.

"Me, too." Cody shifted Noel to his other shoulder. "Here's an idea. Toss out your top three choices and we'll take a vote."

"Noooo," Mandy wailed. "We're not taking a straw poll to name this baby."

"But Mandy," Bryce said, "think of what a great story that would make. And if little whoozit ever complains about his name, you have all of us to blame."

She shook her head. "Not doing it. We'll have one tomorrow, I promise."

"Then let's go with what we've got," Ryker said. "Here's to Zane, Mandy and Baby Whoozit."

Mandy groaned. "Ryker. Honestly."

"What's wrong with that? It's cute."

"It's not cute or original. Besides, you know as well as I do that it could turn into his nickname."

"Over my dead body," Aunt Kendra said.

"And mine." April huffed out a breath. "You need to start over with the toast and put in all the cool stuff you said before about rushing the gate and—"

"Do you want to do it?" Ryker glanced down at her.

"As a matter of fact, I do. I was part of the process today and I've known these guys for years, so I'm highly qualified to propose this toast."

"Go for it."

Aleck stepped forward. "Before we toast, I'd like everyone's permission to follow it up with a pipe and drum number Rory and I talked about. We'll move out to the porch so we don't scare the wee bairn."

"I'd love for you to play," Zane said. "My dad listened to Scottish music all the time. A tune on the pipes and drum will make it seem like he's here, somehow."

Aunt Kendra nodded. "It will, son. That's a lovely thought. What's the song, Aleck?"

"When a Child Is Born."

"Ah, I love that one. It'll make me cry, though."

Quinn wrapped his arm around her shoulders. "You're supposed to cry at times like this."

April delivered her toast, which was much more touching than Ryker's and left folks sniffing and wiping their eyes. Bottles were raised and everyone took a sip of the Baby Brew.

Delicious. As everyone raved about the beer, Aleck lifted his bottle in salute to his brother and Damaris. Rory flashed him a grin of triumph before crossing the room and retrieving his drum.

Aleck picked up the Great Highland pipes and stepped out on the porch with his brother. As he played the first notes of the haunting melody, he gazed at the family members gathered in a semi-circle facing the open door.

Zane stood, ramrod straight, holding his son. His throat moved in a slow swallow and he looked down at Mandy, whose cheeks were wet with tears. Aunt Kendra closed her eyes and leaned against Quinn. Even Ryker looked misty-eyed.

He would get to know all of them better over the next four days. But he would never forget this moment.

<u>6</u>

Tansy had experienced bagpipes before, but she'd never heard them played with such tenderness. She'd enjoyed the rousing music when a pipe band had marched past during parades in Boston, but this tune, typically heard at Christmas, was a lullaby. Aleck's heartfelt rendition wove a spell that stayed with her long after the last note died away.

She happily accepted Kendra's invitation to join their family celebration meal. She'd been out at the ranch plenty of times to ride and she'd attended events here, most recently Ryker and April's wedding. But she'd never sat at the ginormous table in the dining room.

They almost didn't fit, and likely wouldn't have except Mandy confessed she was fading. Zane took their dinner back to the bedroom so they could spend time alone with their son. That left the other four boys and their sweethearts, baby Noel in a highchair, Brendan and Jo, Quinn and Kendra, Rory and Damaris, Aleck and...her.

He invited her to sit next to him and pulled out her chair. Promising. With so much for everyone to discuss—the baby, news from the

Scotland McGavins, the upcoming parade and the festivities afterward, conversation was as plentiful as the food. Sitting next to Aleck for the entire meal was a lovely bonus.

When Kendra asked who was ready for dessert, Bryce and Nicole begged off. "Much as I want some of that pie," Bryce said, "if we leave right now, we'll have time to change clothes before the first set." He pushed back his chair. "Mandy whipped up patriotic outfits for this week's show. I'd thought she'd be coming tonight so she could hear us brag about her work."

"Thanks for that," Jo said. "She gets a lot of business from you guys. I'll tell her you'll be giving her a plug."

"On the other hand," Nicole said, "does she want more business right now?"

"Oh, yes. She's convinced having a baby won't slow her down. I think she's delusional, but I doubt she'll take much time off. She'd miss the creative outlet. Plug away."

"We will, then." Nicole stood. "Great to meet you, Aleck."

"Yeah, cuz," Bryce said. "Awesome sound on the pipes today. Maybe we can work in a jam session with you and Rory while you're here."

"That'd be great."

"Now off you go, kids." Kendra shooed them away from the table.

"Thanks for leaving!" Trevor called after them. "More pie for the rest of us!"

"I'm always thinking of you, Trev!" Bryce grabbed his hat from the coat tree by the door and followed Nicole out.

As everyone helped clear the dishes and bring in the dessert, Tansy waited for Aleck to say something about going to the performance. They had just enough time to eat and still catch the opening number.

Maybe he was too tired, after all, but mentioning it wouldn't hurt anything. Once everyone had dessert, a holiday offering from Pie in the Sky featuring red cherries, blueberries and apples, she spoke up. "Is anybody interested in seeing Bryce and Nicole perform tonight?"

"I am," Aleck said, "but it's been a big day. If I'm the only one, then—"

"You're not," Rory said. "I'd like to go, too. Damaris?"

"I'm up for it."

Right away Trevor, Olivia, Ryker and April jumped on the bandwagon.

"Faith and I will catch it another time," Cody said.

"Grandpa Quinn and I will watch Noel, if that's the issue," Kendra said.

"But then you can't go."

"I won't speak for Quinn, but I'd rather go another night." She used Noel's bib to wipe some applesauce from the little girl's chin.

"Me, too," Quinn said. "Why not let us take Noel across the road to my house?"

"Okay, thanks." Cody smiled. "I guess you two lost your bedroom to the new parents tonight."

"No worries," Kendra said. "We have an alternative. And we're still only five minutes away if they should need us."

"I'm not going to the GG, either." Jo turned to Brendan. "But if you want to, that's—"

"Wouldn't dream of it." He gazed at her. "A granddaddy-in-trainin' doesn't run off to town to drink beer at the local pub." He looked over his shoulder at Quinn. "Right, bro?"

"Right. He drinks beer at home with his favorite grandma, where he's only five minutes away from the grandbaby."

"Exactly," Kendra said. "You two can come over and play cards, though."

"And return phone calls," Quinn said. "I don't know about anybody else, but I promised several people I'd get back to them with details."

"Me, too." Kendra stood. "Time to move out, people."

"Hey, Aleck." Rory got up and started stacking plates. "You should go put on your GG t-shirt. It's in your room on top of the dresser."

"Aye. Good idea. Be right back."

Tansy was carrying the last of the silverware into the kitchen when he reappeared. She almost lost her grip on the bundle of forks and spoons.

Aleck glanced down at the shirt, which fit him like a second skin. "It might be a wee bit small."

"I, um, wouldn't say that."

"No?"

"No." She covered a sigh of pleasure with a quick cough. "I think it's just right."

"Hm." Amusement flickered in his eyes. "If you say so." He held her gaze.

Her stomach executed a few flips. "The logo looks better when the shirt fits smoothly across your...chest."

"I hadn't thought of that."

"It's a marketing thing. You want to be able to easily read—"

"Lookin' good, big brother." Rory came out of the kitchen.

"You don't think it's—"

"Heck, no! Supposed to fit like that. Mine does, and you saw Michael wearing his. Besides, you spend time in the gym. Might as well show off all that hard work."

In an adorable display of modesty, Aleck blushed. "But I don't usually—"

"I know that about you." Rory's voice was gentle. "But take my word for it, the shirt is perfect as is. Just don't put it in hot water."

"I'm about to turn on the dishwasher!" Kendra called from the kitchen. "I'm missing some of the silverware!"

"I have it, Kendra." Tansy hurried through the doorway.

Kendra glanced up from the dishwasher. "You okay?"

"Sure. Why?"

"You have a glazed look in your eyes. I hope you're not coming down with something."

"Aleck put on his shirt."

Kendra's attention shifted to the doorway and she smiled. "I see."

Tansy loaded the silverware. "I didn't realize he was so...so..."

"Built?"

"Uh-huh."

"You have to watch out for those sneaky-sexy guys. Nice smile, polite manner. Seems safe and comfy. Then wham-o, they pull on a tight t-shirt and you go up in flames."

Tansy had never considered Aleck safe and comfortable. He'd stirred her up from the get-go. But the t-shirt cranked up the heat several notches. The fact that he'd never deliberately choose a skin-tight one made the visual even more compelling.

But she had her hormones under control by the time nearly everyone had gathered on the porch before heading to their respective vehicles. Cody and Faith were still organizing Noel's sleepover with her Granny Kendra and Grandpa Quinn.

"I'll give Aleck a ride to the GG," she said. "And bring him back, for that matter."

"Dinna worry about the return trip, lass. I'll just hop in the bed of my brother's truck."

She frowned. "I don't think that's legal."

"It's not," Rory said, "but it wouldn't hurt this one time."

"I suppose." Having him all to herself for the journey each way would have been sweet, though. "See you guys there."

Aleck fell into step beside her as she walked along the line of pickups. Since she'd parked at the end of the row, her little truck was hidden by the bigger rigs everyone else drove.

A growl of thunder caused her to glance up. "Sounds like we might get rain, after all."

"Rory mentioned it. I think he was hopin' somebody would build a fire tonight."

"Wouldn't have been much point with everyone leaving except Zane and Mandy."

"Maybe another night, then. But I'm grateful to you for askin' about the performance." He'd brought his hat and now he settled it on his head as natural as could be. Looked terrific with the black shirt, as Rory had predicted.

"You're welcome. You sounded so excited about it this afternoon that I had to find out if you still wanted to go." Getting him into that t-shirt had been a huge side benefit.

"Oh, I want to go. But nothin' was said when Bryce and Nicole left, so I thought nobody else did."

"Instead, everyone's on board except the grandparents." They reached her truck. "Climb in. It's not locked."

"Rory told us that nobody locks things around here." He stepped over to the driver's side and opened her door. "And he filled me in on cowboy manners."

"I see." She gave him a smile and slid behind the wheel. "Thanks."

"Need to make a good impression since we're representin' our branch of the family."

"You're doing a fabulous job."

"Good to hear, lass." He closed the door and moments later joined her in the compact cab. "Now *this* is cozy." He put his hat in his lap.

It was more like a pressure cooker with his t-shirt covered pecs within easy touching distance. "As opposed to what?" She backed out of the parking space and moved into line behind Rory's truck.

"Wild Creek Ranch. Damaris thinks the layout is cozy, but I beg to differ."

"She's been coming out there since she was a kid. She sees it differently."

"Aye, she told me that. Grew up ridin' horses and cleanin' out stalls for Aunt Kendra. Those barns are huge, though. How many horses live here?"

His questions sounded casual even though awareness crackled in the air. But if he could pretend to be oblivious, so could she. "The number changes since some are boarders, but I'd estimate between thirty-five and forty."

"See? That's not a few animals. That's a herd."

"I agree, but without that many, Kendra wouldn't make enough to sustain the ranch operation. She needs a certain number of boarders and enough of her own horses to make up the weekend trail rides."

"How many people does it take to run the operation?"

Maybe asking questions was his way of diffusing the heat of their attraction. "Well, let's see. Kendra and Zane are the head honchos. Cody and Faith contribute a lot, too, although they've cut back some since Noel was born. Faith's dad, Jim Underwood, is the foreman."

"He wasn't there today, was he?"

"No. Might have had the day off."

"I saw the horses out in the pasture when Rory and I drove in. Can they live on whatever grass they find?"

"That's not enough for them. They get fed hay every morning and evening, plus grain now and then."

"Who did it today?"

"Good question." And he sure was full of them. "I guarantee someone went down there, likely two somebodies. My money's on Trevor and Brendan."

"Why?"

"Trevor's in construction these days and a volunteer firefighter, but he grew up on the ranch. He could do the feeding routine blindfolded. Brendan's good with any kind of animal, wild or domestic. You could ask Trevor how the horses got fed."

"I just might do that."

"I can't help noticing that you have a lot of questions about this way of life."

He flashed her a grin. "Askin' questions is second nature to me. It's how I make my livin'."

"Yes, but—"

"It's also my knee-jerk response to somethin' that's completely foreign to me. When I'm out of my depth, I Hoover up everythin' I can."

"Fair enough."

"I'm happy so many are goin' tonight. Gives me a chance to buy a round. I'm very good at orderin' beer."

"Good luck with that. You might have to arm-wrestle a couple of McGavins first."

"That could be interestin'. I used to do quite a bit of that. Haven't lately. I think I could take Cody, possibly Trevor, but if they put me up against Ryker, chances are I'm goin' down."

"It's his military bearing."

"Nay, it's his muscles. He's built for the caber toss."

"I don't know what that is, but if it involves brute strength, Ryker's up to it."

"The caber toss is one of the main events in the Highland games."

"And a caber is…"

"A log the size of a telephone pole."

"Wow. Have you ever done it?"

"Oh, yeah. Rory and I had to prove ourselves to be manly men." He chuckled. "Can't say we did it well, but we did it. Caber toss, hammer throw, shot put. We gave them all a go."

"Wearing kilts?"

"Aye. That's how it's done."

"Any videos?" Surely someone had recorded that for posterity.

"God, I hope not."

Damn. "Listen, if you've managed to toss a telephone pole without injuring yourself, you shouldn't take a back seat to any of these cowboys."

"Aye, but I've never ridden a horse, now, have I?"

"You'd be fine."

"That's what Rory says."

"It's no different from the caber toss and that other stuff you mentioned. You do it so you can say you did."

"Are you throwin' down a gauntlet, lass?" He sounded amused.

"I might be. I'm on the evening shift for the next few days so my days are free. How about going for a ride with me?"

"Well..."

"I dare you."

He started laughing.

"I double-dog dare you."

Now he was laughing so hard he could barely talk. "Never heard that one." He gulped for air. "Sounds...very...serious."

"Oh, it is. You don't back down from a double-dog dare unless you want to lose your manly man standing."

Clearing his throat, he glanced over at her. "You win. I'll go ridin'."

Victory.

7

Several fat drops of rain fell on the asphalt as Aleck walked across the Guzzling Grizzly parking lot with Tansy. The wind had picked up enough that he had to hold his hat to keep it from flying off.

A streak of lightning preceded an ear-splitting boom and the crisp scent of ozone. Instinct took over. Wrapping a protective arm around Tansy, he hustled her toward the entrance. They hurtled through the door as another flash lit up the night and thunder crackled overhead.

The pending storm gave way to a happy babble of voices. Canned country music was on the sound system, which meant they'd made it before Bryce and Nicole's first number.

"Yikes." Tansy gave him a smile. "Thanks for protecting me."

"You're welcome." He let her go, but the warmth from that brief contact lingered. He wanted more of that. The ride in her wee cab, breathing in her scent, had nearly undone him. Firing questions had been his only defense.

But he might as well raise the white flag and get it over with. Involvement with Tansy made no sense whatsoever, and he lived his life by logic. Or he had before walking into the Guzzling Grizzly and gazing into those warm brown eyes.

When other guys had told him about a similar reaction to a woman, he'd scoffed. Yeah, sure, made a terrific story, but it wasn't based in any kind of reality. The joke was on him.

"Hey, there, Tansy!" The blonde woman's nametag identified her as Ellen. "Can't remember the last time you came through the front door."

"I can. When I applied for a job here. Ellen, meet Aleck, Rory's big brother."

"Aleck! I should have guessed. It's so good to meet you at last."

"Nice to meet you, too, Ellen." He soaked in the cheerful ambiance of the nighttime crowd. The venue was larger and brighter than most Scottish pubs, but the mood was the same. No wonder Rory loved it. A pub suited him much better than a lab.

"The GG shirt looks great on you, by the way."

"Thank you." He'd never worn a t-shirt this snug. It had a curious effect on him, especially when he caught Tansy looking at his chest with obvious appreciation. Her admiration ignited a sensuality he hadn't acknowledged before. He wanted to explore it.

"Follow me," Ellen said. "The table is as close to the stage as we could manage. It's an eight-top, but we've squeezed in two extra chairs."

"Good work." Tansy followed her over to a round table set for ten.

Ryker, April, Trevor, Olivia, Rory and Damaris were already there. The men stood at their approach but the women stayed seated. Evidently that was protocol for this venue. Rory had advised him that when in doubt, stand up. A man couldn't commit too many social errors in Eagles Nest if he got to his feet anytime something new transpired.

"You beat the storm!" Rory gave them a broad smile. "I hate to say it, Tansy, but you might need to take this crazy brother of mine home, after all. I'd rather not have him get struck by lightnin' while hunkered down in the back of my pickup."

"I'm opposed to that idea, myself." A ride home in her truck would be a bonnie solution to the transportation issue and might give him a chance to kiss her goodnight.

After he and Tansy grabbed a seat, he glanced around the table. "Have you ordered?"

"We have," Rory said. "We got a round of McGavin's Pale Ale for everyone. Figured that was a safe bet."

"Much obliged. The next round's on me."

"Appreciate the offer, but you're a guest." Ryker said it as if that took care of the matter.

"Aye, but that doesn't mean I can't—"

"Yes, it does, big brother." Rory glanced at him. "I bought my first round of drinks for these folks after I came to live here and lost my guest privileges."

"I can vouch for that," Tansy said. "I've been observing this bunch for a while, now. When they come here en masse, which happens a lot, they have a mysterious rotating system for who gets the bill. But it's never the guest."

"I see. So that thing you said about arm wrestlin' one of the McGavins for the bill was—"

"I was just kidding. They don't really do that."

Ryker's eyebrows lifted. "Unless you *want* to give that a shot. I'd be glad to accommodate you."

"Maybe not tonight. Bein' jet-lagged and all."

"Bet you could take him." Rory's quiet comment was filled with brotherly pride.

Aleck winced. "Thanks for the vote of confidence, but I—"

"You arm wrestle?" Ryker sat up straighter.

"I have, yes."

"Are you any good?"

"Well, I—"

"He's very good." Rory pretended not to notice that Damaris was gently elbowing him in the ribs. "Never lost a match that I remember. Uses psychology."

"Is that right?" Ryker's eyes lit with interest.

"Psychology is a fine thing," Trevor said, "but my money would still be on Ryker. No offense, Aleck, but you don't have quite the…"

"Muscle mass?" Aleck smiled. "I'm aware of that. Besides, I spend my days sitting in a courtroom while Ryker…"

"I sit in a cockpit, which isn't any better." Ryker shrugged. "I work out some, though. How about you?"

"Some. Probably not at your level. I'm not planning to challenge you."

"Okay. But if you change your mind, let me know. I'm always up for a match."

"That's the truth." Trevor looked over at Aleck. "He has trouble finding opponents."

"I'm not surprised."

"Are we talking about Ryker's domination of the arm-wrestling scene?" Cody arrived with Faith and they took the remaining two chairs at the table.

"I hope not for much longer." Ryker grimaced. "I can't imagine a more boring subject."

"It's monotonous, for sure," Trevor said. "I can't remember the last time someone beat you, either."

"I'm trying to think if anyone ever has." Cody glanced up as Ellen and another server approached with mugs of beer. "McGavin's Pale Ale, incoming. Thanks for ordering, guys."

"Yeah, thanks," Faith said. "I'm glad we're doing this. Nicole and Bryce worked so hard on this show. I can't wait to see it." She turned to Aleck. "They'll blow you away."

"Aye, I'm sure of it."

"I propose a toast," April said.

Ryker chuckled. "Somebody's got the toasting bug."

"I do! I can't imagine why I haven't been more assertive about claiming toasting privileges." She lifted her mug. "Here's to Bryce and Nicole's new show and to Aleck for paying us a visit. May it be the first of many."

Rory lifted his mug in Aleck's direction. "The first of many. All in favor, give me an *aye*."

"*Aye!*" Their raised voices caused several customers to turn in their direction.

"Oh, darn, we're attracting attention." Cody grinned. "I hate it when that happens."

"It's good to make some noise," April said. "We want Bryce and Nicole to know we're out here. When they left the house, we didn't say we'd be coming."

"And we wouldn't have if Tansy hadn't spoken up." Faith turned to her. "Thanks for that."

"You're welcome."

"I was afraid Cody and I would be late, but we got here faster than usual. They won't be out for another fifteen minutes."

"I guess we could dance." Olivia swiveled in her chair to check out the situation. "Forget that. The floor's packed. I'll just sit and enjoy my wonderful pale ale."

"It's great, all right," Trevor said. "I can't decide which I like better, this or McGavin's Baby Brew." He hoisted his mug in Rory's direction. "Good job, buddy."

More similar comments followed from everyone else at the table.

"Thanks." Rory looked pleased with the compliments and Aleck was pleased for him. Good vibes.

Trevor took a deep swallow, set down his mug and gazed at Rory. "Now I can't get the idea out of my head."

Rory looked puzzled. "What idea?"

"A battle of the undefeated. Your brother and mine. We have enough time before the show starts. I'd love to see it."

"Ah. So would I, but—"

"Aleck isn't up to it, Trev." Ryker sent him a warning glance. "He's tired from his trip. Don't push it."

Rory sighed. "Aye, you have the right of it. Now's not the time."

"I agree," Tansy said. "The poor guy got off a plane only a few hours ago. He had a long flight, and despite that, he summoned the energy to give us a wonderful bagpipe concert. That had to be taxing. I'll bet he's exhausted."

"Not that exhausted." Aleck had heard enough. He didn't want any of them, least of all Tansy, viewing him as a *poor guy* who couldn't handle an overseas flight and a few tunes on the bagpipe without turning into a limp dishrag of a man. He glanced across the table. "Ryker, it's on."

Ryker's expression changed from relaxed to alert. "Now?"

"Aye. Tansy, if you'd please trade places with Ryker, we can—"

"Seriously, Aleck?" She looked at him as if he'd lost his mind.

"Might as well."

She gazed at him with a mixture of concern and admiration. "Boys." Then she picked up her mug and walked over to the chair Ryker had just vacated.

Her concern was nice, but it was her admiration he was going for. Chances were good he'd lose to Ryker, who had biceps the size of watermelons. But he wouldn't go down easy. Laying his hat on the table, he moved his beer mug and repositioned his chair.

Ryker left his hat with April and came over to sit in Tansy's chair. "I almost hate to accept this challenge, Aleck. Doesn't seem fair."

"Don't worry about me." Adrenaline pumped through his system as he met Ryker's gaze. "I can take care of myself." He positioned his elbow on the table.

A gleam of respect flashed in Ryker's eyes. "You have guts, buddy." He mirrored Aleck's position and flexed his fingers.

"Runs in the family."

"So it does. Who wants to referee?"

"I'll start you off." Cody got up and came around to their side of the table. "But you guys know the rules. We don't need no stinkin' referee."

"Aye, right," Rory said. "This is just a friendly match."

Ryker clasped Aleck's hand. "Exactly. A little diversion to pass the time."

Like hell. Ryker's body language projected laser-like focus. A decent showing against the guy would take everything he had and it still might not be enough. He drew in a deep breath and tightened his grip.

"Okay." Cody put his hand over their joined ones. "On three. One, two, *three.*" He let go.

Dear God. Aleck sucked in a breath as Ryker attacked with a vengeance, dragging his wrist almost to the table's surface.

Almost. Aleck's neck and shoulder muscles screamed in protest as he abruptly halted the downward trajectory. And began to reverse it.

His opponent's grin of satisfaction faded and his mighty chest heaved as he bore down again. Aleck held his ground and gained another millimeter. Ryker's eyes widened.

Surprise! I'm not dead yet! Ryker's astonishment spurred him on as he began the Herculean task of regaining the territory he'd lost, millimeter by agonizing millimeter.

Jaw clenched and breathing hard, he blinked away the sweat blurring his vision. Maintaining eye contact was half the battle. Beads of sweat popped out on Ryker's brow, too. Gratifying.

A wee bit more. Almost there...ahh. Back in control. Time to play offense. Aye, right. Easier said than done. He'd have better luck shoving the Guzzling Grizzly off its foundation than budging that massive fist.

Ryker spoke through clenched teeth. "Thought you didn't work out much." He increased the pressure.

Aleck dug deep and held him off. "I don't." His lungs burned as he struggled for enough oxygen to maintain his position.

"Then how the hell..."

He managed a grim smile. "Bagpipes."

8

By changing places with Ryker, Tansy ended up staring at his broad back but looking straight at Aleck as the match began. Other than startled exclamations from the group at the table after Ryker's first move and a few gasps as Aleck fought his way back, everyone stayed quiet.

Made sense. Ryker was a local hero but Aleck was a special visitor from Scotland, Rory's big brother. How could anyone choose a side?

Well, except for Rory. He watched the competition with fierce intensity, but didn't say anything. Probably didn't want to risk breaking Aleck's concentration.

Gradually a crowd gathered around the table, but those folks didn't make any comments, either. Even the country music on the sound system had been turned off. Everyone in the GG seemed to be holding a collective breath as each man struggled to overcome the other.

Aleck's chest and arm muscles bulged, straining against the black cotton of his t-shirt. Tansy's line-of-sight gave her a ringside view of his rigid jaw, bared teeth and the unholy fire burning in his eyes.

This was not the smiling Scot she'd served a mug of beer this afternoon or the sensitive piper who'd serenaded his kinfolk with a lullaby for a newborn. This man was a Highland warrior. And Ryker had met his match.

"Good evening." Bryce's mellow voice came through the large speakers on the stage.

Tansy glanced in that direction, then at the time on her phone. The show should have started five minutes ago.

Bryce stood next to the mic, his stance casual, his smile relaxed. "What do you say we call it a draw?"

Aleck and Ryker remained frozen in place for another couple of seconds before relaxing their grip in unison and smiling at each other. As they stood and shook hands, the onlookers cheered.

Ryker pulled a bandana out of his back pocket and mopped his brow. Rory dug out his and handed it to Aleck, who likely didn't have a single bandana to his name. Yet.

"Now if y'all will take a seat," Bryce said, "I'll go fetch my lady and we'll make a proper entrance."

"Sorry if we held up the show, Bryce!" Aleck called out.

"Not a problem, cuz! That was mighty fine entertainment. You and Ryker can open for us anytime."

Beer mug in hand, Tansy returned to her seat in time to catch Aleck and Ryker discussing a rematch.

"Guys, guys." She shook her head. "Please don't stage a rematch. Be content with a draw, okay?"

"But we didn't settle anything," Ryker said.

"Why do you have to? This outcome is way better. You're both winners."

"Good luck selling them on that one," April called over to her.

"I'm gonna try, but not now. It's show time." She turned her chair to face the stage and Aleck did the same.

He leaned close. "Didn't think we'd take that long. Dinna mean to delay the show."

"I'm guessing you forgot everything but the match." She took a sip of her beer and set it behind her on the table.

"Aye. That I did."

"For the record, I'm impressed."

"Are you, now?" He combed his damp hair back from his forehead.

"Very impressed."

He grinned. "That's worth a wee bit of sweatin'."

"Oh?" Had he done it partly for her? The intro to Kenny Chesney's *American Kids* stopped her from asking the question.

Nicole and Bryce came out rocking that song, one of Tansy's favorites. Red and blue sequins that decorated their white Western shirts flashed in the lights and Nicole's curly red hair was barely contained by her white Stetson.

She took both hands off her guitar and started rhythmically clapping. "Come on, folks, sing it with me!"

Tansy threw herself into the number, clapping along with the crowd and singing at the top of her lungs. Beside her, Aleck rested his right hand on his thigh, indicating the match had taken its toll. But he tapped out the rhythm with his left hand.

By the second chorus he was belting out the words in his distinctive Scottish brogue. Her heart warmed. Despite having no reason to celebrate an American holiday, he was clearly going all in.

The number ended and the crowd roared their approval. She glanced over at Aleck and he was cheering louder than everyone.

As the racket faded and Nicole took the lead with Faith Hill's *American Heart,* Aleck turned to her. "Thank you for makin' this happen."

"I didn't do anything."

"Sure you did." He reached for her hand and squeezed it. Then he laced his fingers through hers.

Nicole's voice flowed over her, enhancing the energy of their linked hands. She never wanted the song to end. When it did, he slipped his hand from hers so she could applaud and he could do his best by slapping his thigh.

She leaned toward him. "I notice you're not using your right hand."

"It'll be fine in a while."

"Did you challenge Ryker partly to impress me?"

He chuckled. "First off, Rory wanted me to and I was also gettin' sick of everyone mollycoddlin' me. But mostly I wanted to impress you."

"I hope you realize I already think you're special."

His eyes sparkled with amusement. "Meanin' that was overkill?"

"Not at all. I just—" She discontinued the discussion since Nicole had handed her guitar to Bryce and stepped up to the mic holding a handful of Mandy's business cards. "We'll talk later."

"Countin' on it."

Her breath caught. Unless she was mistaken, he was looking forward to being alone with her. The glittering prospect of quality time with Aleck at the end of the evening kept her from giving her full attention to Nicole.

She rededicated herself to the task because she was a huge fan of Mandy's custom clothing. She owned several of her creations.

"I know you're all admiring our shirts and wishing you could have one just like it," Nicole said. "And you can! Check out Mandy McGavin's artistry." She executed a slow turn so everyone could see a rippling American flag portrayed in sequins on the back. "Can I have an *oooo*?" The audience responded. "Now give me an *ahhhh*."

Tansy's *ahhhh* was enthusiastic. "I love sequins," she said as Nicole came down from the stage and began handing out business cards.

"Is that so?"

"Crazy for them. A logo shirt decorated with sequins would be awesome. Mandy's willing to make it, but if I wear a shirt with bling, customers will want one. The guys aren't sure Mandy can keep up with the orders."

"Especially with a bairn to take care of."

"Exactly. I've suggested hiring someone to help, maybe even a couple of people. She agrees in principle, but ironically she's too busy to take time for the hiring process and quality control is super important to her."

"Sounds like she needs a trusty business manager to handle that kind of thing."

"She does if she wants to grow, but she doesn't have time to look for that person, either. It needs to be someone she knows, ideally from here."

"How about you?"

She stared at him. "I already have a job."

"Aye, but..." He paused and shook his head. "Never mind."

"What?"

"Ignore me. I have older brother syndrome. Do you have any older brothers?"

"Three."

"Then you know what I'm talkin' about."

"But you're not my brother."

"Saints be praised. Otherwise I'd be headin' straight to hell for my inappropriate thoughts."

She smiled. "That would make two of us." The strum of guitars signaled that the short commercial break was over. She faced forward again, but her peripheral vision was excellent, one of the many reasons she was a good bartender.

Aleck kept glancing her way. Clearly he enjoyed the view.

She was fine with that. When he took her hand during the next slow tune, she laced her fingers snugly with his. Each time a number ended they had to let go so they could clap and cheer. Eventually, as if by mutual agreement, they held hands during every song that wasn't a clap-along.

Toward the end of the show, Nicole and Bryce introduced an original patriotic composition titled *Say Yes.* Tansy agreed with the song's message—say yes to the country's ideals and act on them. But when Aleck held her hand and stroked it with his thumb, she was ready to say yes in a whole other context.

The grand finale featured Bryce and Nicole performing *America the Beautiful* while a video of breathtaking scenes scrolled across the wall behind them. Nicole invited everyone to sing along and Tansy did. Aleck didn't and she respected that. The song wasn't the national anthem, but it was in anthem territory. He stood when everyone else did, though.

After the show, Bryce and Nicole came over to thank everyone for coming.

"Thank Tansy," Faith said. "She got the ball rolling."

"Well, Aleck said this show was at the top of his list, so naturally I—"

"Yeah?" Bryce turned to him. "I'm honored."

"Hey, you two are great. I've been hooked ever since Rory sent me your latest album. I've played it for a few people and you have a fan club developing over there. If you ever want to tour in Scotland, I'd be happy to set one up."

"We'd love to." Nicole exchanged a glance with Bryce. "We'd relay that message to our business manager except we still haven't hired one."

Tansy smiled at Aleck. "As you can see, it's a common problem in these parts."

"I'm gettin' that."

"Anyway, we're going home." Nicole gestured toward the ceiling. "From the sound of it, we're getting quite a bit of rain. We need to check on the cat. He gets nervous when it rains hard."

Tansy had been so absorbed by the show and Aleck that she'd missed the steady pounding on the roof of the GG. "I guess it is coming down pretty good out there."

"Luckily we parked by the back entrance so we won't have to go far." Bryce turned toward the stage. "The band should be set up soon if you want to stay and wait it out."

"I'm for that," Cody said. "No need to rush home since the folks offered to keep Noel overnight."

"Yeah, I'd like to hang out here a while." April looked over at Ryker, who nodded in agreement.

"We'll stay, too," Olivia said. "I haven't danced with Trevor in ages."

"Same with me and Damaris." Rory glanced at Aleck. "But you probably want to head home, big brother."

"Aye. I'm startin' to fade."

"Let's vamoose." Tansy grabbed her small purse from her seat. "I'm sure a Scotsman can handle a few drops of rain."

"That's for sure."

But when they opened the GG's front door, sheets of rain poured off the roof as if they were standing behind a waterfall.

Aleck drew her back inside. "You know what? That's more than a few drops of rain. You don't have to go out in it since you live upstairs. I'll just call a cab."

"That's an excellent idea except for one teensy problem."

"What's that?"

"There's no cab service in Eagles Nest."

"Oh."

"I'd invite you up to my apartment to rest your weary head, but that's a bold step."

"Aye." He scrubbed a hand over his face. "Temptin' as that is, I wouldn't be comfortable with it."

"It's just water." She pulled out her keys. "I'll beep open the locks from here and we'll make a run for it."

"Will the rain ruin this hat Rory bought me?"

"Not if we set it brim-side up to dry once we're in the house."

His eyes lit up. "You're coming in?"

"Unless you don't want me to."

"Oh, I want you to, lass."

Adrenaline shot through her system. "But you're tired."

"Not that tired."

"Then let's go."

9

By the time Aleck wrenched open the passenger door of Tansy's wee truck, he was soaked to the skin. "I'm drippin' all over your seat, lass."

"It'll dry. Don't worry about it." She started the engine and turned on the wipers. "At least the rain was warm."

"It did feel like takin' a shower with my clothes on. I have water in my boots, too. My toes are squishin' inside there."

"We'll pour the water out and see if Kendra has some old newspapers to stuff in them." She backed out of the parking space and drove slowly toward the parking lot exit. "I think I saw a basket of papers near the fireplace."

"Aye, there was." He watched the wipers struggle to handle the water. "Can you see out your windscreen?"

"Windscreen? Oh, you mean windshield. The visibility's not great, but I'll take it easy down this road. Nobody else is out here, thankfully."

"Except Bryce and Nicole."

"They're not on this road. They're headed back into town. Nicole inherited a beautiful

Victorian house from her great aunt and they live there."

"With a cat?"

Tansy laughed. "He's more like a force of nature. Nicole inherited him along with the house. I expect by now that cat is lounging in front of the cozy fire they built for him."

"A blazin' fire would be braw after gettin' rained on."

"Braw means good?"

"Aye, but I wasn't suggestin' it for us. Not without askin'."

"And asking means disturbing Zane and Mandy."

"Canna be doin' that." The rain came down in torrents, blotting out the landscape, enclosing them in a watery cocoon. "First night with a new bairn. Wonder what that's like for them."

"I can't imagine."

"Rory's already talkin' about havin' a family. He said in another year or two, I'll be an uncle. Canna fathom that."

"I'm an aunt."

"Truly?"

"Truly. Seven times over. All my brothers are married with kids."

"Do you see them often?"

"I've gone back twice since moving here. It's...weird."

"How?"

"They all act like my decision to live in Eagles Nest is a phase I'll outgrow. They don't say that to my face, but Cameron, who's seven, told me straight out—*Daddy says you just have to get this out of your system.*"

"Let me guess. Cameron's da is your eldest brother."

"Bingo. Thinks he knows what's best for everyone."

"Must be annoyin'." And he'd delivered the same claptrap to Rory more times than he could count. At least he hadn't made the mistake of treating his brother's Montana plan as a phase. That would have seriously strained their relationship.

"It's very annoying. I'm nothing like my brothers. My birth certificate says I'm Mom and Dad's biological child or I'd swear I was adopted."

Good thing he'd reined in his advice-giving impulse earlier tonight. He'd been on the brink of saying that tending bar at the GG wasn't a growth position, whereas offering her services as a business manager had a future. She had two potential clients within easy reach.

If he'd finished that arrogant speech instead of thinking better of it, he'd have come off sounding just like her patronizing brother. He had even less reason to state an opinion. What she did with her life was none of his damn business.

Ah, but he was curious about what she'd rebelled against. "What do they expect you to do once you get this out of your system?"

"Go back to school, get my law degree, join the family practice."

"Ah. Solicitors, are they?" Now he was *really* glad he'd kept his mouth shut. Between his older brother status and his profession, he could be tarred with the pompous ass brush in no time.

"Yep. Dad started the firm and he's semi-retired now that the boys are on board."

"Given all that, I'm surprised you've had anythin' to do with me."

She smiled. "I wouldn't have if you'd come into the GG without the hat and boots."

"I almost did."

"What changed your mind?"

"You haven't figured that out?"

"I have a theory, but I could be wrong."

"I wanted to make Rory happy."

"I *knew* it. You abandoned logic because you love your brother."

"Aye. It finally registered that outfittin' me in a hat and boots meant the world to him."

"I'm sure it did. Hang on. I'm coming up on the ranch road. It'll be muddy. We might do some sliding."

"I'm prepared." Although she made the turn at a snail's pace, her wee truck fishtailed anyway and he grabbed the armrest to steady himself.

"Sorry about that." She got the bonnet pointed in the right direction and continued down the road. "Slippery out there."

"Now I'm thinkin' about you drivin' back down this road alone. What if you end up in a ditch?"

"I'll call George's Garage. They have a tow truck."

"Would they come get you in the middle of the night in the rain?"

"Probably."

"That's not the ringing affirmative I was lookin' for."

"I won't get stuck. Even if I do, I have a bunch of people I could call. Rory and Damaris will pass this way to get home and so will Cody and Faith. It's not like I'd be stranded for hours."

"I don't want you stranded for five minutes, let alone hours."

"Look, it's not going to happen so there's no reason to keep talking about it. I'd rather hear more about the hat and boots. He told me he was planning to pay for them. Did you let him?"

"I had to after he proudly announced he was making decent money and could afford it." He'd switch topics for now, but the discussion wasn't over. "That's another reason I want to make sure the rain didn't do any damage. I plan to have these items a very long time."

"You two really are close. It's a shame you live so far apart, now."

"I miss him like the devil. When I take home the hat and boots, I'll be takin' home a reminder of my brother. Makes me wonder why I argued so hard against buyin' 'em. Pure stubbornness, I guess."

"And maybe habit? After all, arguing your side, or your client's side, is how you make your living."

"Aye, right." He glanced at her. "I guess you would be very familiar with that habit."

"Ohh, yeah. Our family dinner table conversation was something to behold. Five people in the house loved it, calling it a *stimulating environment.*"

"But you hated it."

"I didn't understand that for the longest time. I thought I just needed to get better at debate. Law school would teach me how to hold my own. Then the light dawned. I had no interest in getting better at debate so I could hold my own in those family free-for-alls. So I dropped out."

"And went to bartending school?"

"I did, but I had the job first and the training later. I faked my way through the first six months because I'd become friends with the owner when I was a student."

"What school?"

"Harvard."

"Hey, now."

"I know. A girl who turns her back on a Harvard education is either crazy or stupid, right?"

"I wouldn't consider you either of those things, lass."

"Thanks. I wasted a lot of my parents' money, though. I've paid most of it back, although they haven't cashed a single check I've sent them."

"They're savin' it for when you get this out of your system."

"That's my guess, too, although the smart thing would be to bank it and at least collect some interest."

"That wouldn't send much of a message. Not cashing the checks is more dramatic."

"There you go. Gamesmanship. I'm no good at that, either. Okay, brace yourself. We have another curve to navigate and then we'll be there."

He gripped the armrest. Good thing, because the truck swerved a couple of times before she got it straightened out. She wasn't driving back tonight alone and that was final.

At the end of the road, the outline of the ranch buildings was blurred by the heavy rain. Dusk to dawn lights cast a faint glow from the barn area.

"I'll park as close to the walkway as I can without knocking over a fence."

"I appreciate the effort, but I'm still soaked. If I pick up more moisture on the way to the house, I doubt I'll notice."

"Okay." She brought the truck to a halt when it was even with the flagstone path leading to the porch. "Looks like someone left some lights on in the living room. At least we won't be stumbling around in the dark."

"Guess not." Although he wouldn't have minded. Stumbling around in the dark had possibilities.

"Kendra has hardwood floors, so we won't want to stand and drip in one place. One large puddle does more damage to the floor than several smaller ones, so just keep moving toward the kitchen and on into the laundry room. We'll mop up later."

"Got it. Sounds like the way Ma used to organize us when we managed to get wet and muddy."

"If you stick to the flagstone path, you shouldn't get muddy."

"But it's safe to say your wee purple truck is covered with it."

She shrugged that off. "It's happened before. When we leave the truck, make a dash for the porch. Don't wait for me. Just go for it."

"And then what?"

"We'll rendezvous when we get there, maybe empty our boots before we go inside. Then we'll...wait a minute." She rolled down her window about an inch. "Aha! I thought I smelled smoke. Zane must have made a fire. You'll get to sit in front of a blazing hearth after all."

"I hope they're not havin' difficulties with the bairn."

"You and me, both. What I know about babies would fit on the bottom of a shot glass. Maybe they just wanted the ambiance on this rainy night. We'll find out."

"Aye." But one thing was certain. The kiss he'd been hoping to steal at the end of this journey had just been denied him.

<u>10</u>

Tansy had looked forward to having the living room to themselves, but that wasn't to be. Tucking her keys in her small purse, she glanced at Aleck. "Ready?"

"If you are."

"Meet you on the porch." She scrambled out of the truck and ran around the hood to the walkway, her boots splashing through water and mud. They'd be a mess, but at least Aleck's wouldn't take the same abuse.

He made it to the porch ahead of her. As she ran up the steps to join him, the front door opened and Zane came out.

He was barefoot and wearing an unbuttoned shirt over a worn pair of jeans. "Thought I heard somebody drive up. Rain's coming down so hard I wasn't sure."

"We're a mess." Tansy gestured to her boots and mud-spattered jeans. "Especially me. I don't want to get your mom's floor dirty."

"I'll get some towels. Be right back." He ducked through the door. "Honey, it's Aleck and Tansy," he called out. "I'm getting them some towels and stuff."

"Okay." Mandy's voice came from the back of the house. "I'll be out in a minute with Rhys."

Tansy glanced at Aleck and grinned. "Did we just hear the name they picked for the baby?"

"I believe we did, lass."

"We could be the first ones to know."

"I'd bet on it."

"That's kinda cool." She gestured to the rockers on the porch. "They're wet, but so are we. Have a seat so you can take off your boots."

"Aye, right."

She took the rocker next to his. "Ugh. Mine are covered in mud. I'm gonna try to get them off without touching them." Bracing the toe of one boot against the heel of the other, she worked her foot out.

Repeating the process on the other side meant getting her sock muddy, but at least her hands stayed clean. After pulling off her clean sock, she used it to remove the muddy one. "Done."

"Me, too. I can't remember the last time I was this wet." Aleck wrung out his socks and laid them over the arm of the rocker. "Pretty toes you have there."

"Thanks." She looked down and wiggled them. She'd alternated red, white and blue for Independence Day. "Those colors would look awful in my hair, although I considered it. I settled on making my toes patriotic, even if hardly anybody will know since I wear boots most of the time."

"Well, I know and I'll think of your toes even if you're wearin' boots."

"That sounds kinky."

His eyes sparkled in the glow of the porch light. "Aye, it does, doesn't it?"

"You have nice toes, too."

He laughed. "Dinna think anybody's ever said that to me."

"It's true, though. Some men's feet aren't great to look at, but yours are nice."

"I've got supplies!" Zane appeared with his arms full.

"Thanks so much." Tansy met him by the door and relieved him of the towels. "Glad you brought plenty." She glanced at what else he'd carried out. "Did you bring clothes?"

"For you. Mandy donated a pair of her sweats and a t-shirt."

"She doesn't need them?" She handed two towels to Aleck.

"Nope. When Aunt Jo and Uncle Brendan brought back the stuff for the delivery, they also loaded up on extra clothes for Mandy and me. We probably have enough for three or four days, but we won't be here that long."

"Then I'll be happy to accept the loan." She wiped the nearest rocker with one of her towels and draped it over the back. "You can set them right there."

"Good deal." He laid the bundle on the chair and turned to Aleck. "Hey, buddy, if you don't mind me rummaging through your suitcase, I could bring you some dry clothes, too. Changing out here will keep the water and mud to a minimum."

"It's brilliant. If you'd bring me a t-shirt and jeans, that'll do it. Oh, and a pair of briefs. I'm soaked clear through."

Tansy sighed. "So am I. I don't suppose Mandy—"

"She tucked a pair of panties in with the t-shirt and sweats. And a camisole."

"Perfect."

"Then I'll fetch Aleck's clothes." He started toward the door.

"Wait." Aleck took off his hat. "Would you please take this and my boots in for me? Tansy said the hat will be okay if it dries brim side up."

"It will. I'll put it in a safe spot. And I'll stuff some newspaper into your boots."

"Much obliged."

"Happy to help out. Be back in a sec with your clothes."

"Well, now." Tansy gazed at Aleck. "Undressing out on the front porch. Is that a new one for you?"

"Nay, do it all the time."

She smiled. "I'm so sure. How are you holding up?"

"Are you askin' if I'm ready to drop from exhaustion?"

"Yes."

"Not yet. I'd like to sit in front of that fire for a bit. And I also—"

"Here you go." Zane came back out and handed over Aleck's clothes. "I'll leave you guys to it." He started back in. "Oh, Mandy said to tell you she's making hot chocolate. Do either of you want some?"

"I do," Tansy said.

"Sounds great."

"Good. I'll tell her." He went in and closed the door.

Aleck gazed at her. "I've never done this in my life."

"Neither have I."

"How about if I go to the end of the porch and you stay here?"

"Afraid I'll jump you?"

He chuckled. "I only wish."

"Tempting as you are, I can't see myself doing that when there's a potential audience inside the house and the possibility of someone driving up. You don't have to go *all* the way to the end of the porch. Halfway will work."

"Okay." He started down the row of chairs, paused in front of one and wiped it off with one of his towels. "And I promise I won't look."

"I won't, either."

"Then you might want to turn around." He started pulling off his shirt.

Much as she hated to, she did. She was a woman of her word, damn it. "Are you facing away from me, now?"

"Aye. Like a good boy."

"Alrighty, then."

"You know, I see what Rory means." Aleck pitched his voice low, which made it sound even sexier than usual.

"About what?" She rubbed a towel quickly over her hair.

"The way this family takes care of each other. My family's the same."

"I gathered that." She pulled her t-shirt over her head and tossed it on the arm of the rocker. After a moment's hesitation, she took off her wet bra, laid it over her t-shirt and toweled off.

"There's not as many of us," he continued in the same easy tone, "but we watch out for each other like this, too."

"That's nice." Talking to him while topless was a combo guaranteed to ignite lust. She quickly located the camisole in the pile of clothes and pulled it over her sensitized breasts. "Does that mean you'll need to make lots of trips over here?"

"I'm thinkin' so." The buzz of a zipper meant he was shucking his jeans.

"Rory will be glad to hear that." She pulled the t-shirt over her head.

"Are you?"

"I'm thinkin' so." She unfastened her jeans and shoved them off along with her panties.

"This is pure torture."

"Is it?" She pretended not to know what he meant as she grabbed the towel and made quick work of drying off. Being half naked with a gorgeous man only a few feet away, one she wasn't supposed to approach but desperately wanted to, was indeed torture.

"I heard you takin' off your jeans and I'm..."

"You're what?"

"Havin' trouble zippin' mine."

"Wish I could help you out."

"Wish you could, too." He took a deep breath. "Done. Are you?"

"No. Will be in a minute."

"Need any help?"

"Not now. But when I do, you'll be the first to know."

His soft groan was music to her ears.

_11_

Much more of that routine and Aleck would have recommended himself for sainthood. A perfectly logical plan had quickly transformed into a hormonal catastrophe. He never wanted to do such a thing again.

When he was finally allowed to turn around, he had to stand still for a minute and catch his breath while he gazed at Tansy. Otherwise he would have marched down that porch and kissed her.

Her hair was tousled as if she'd been rolling around in bed doing the kinds of things that he'd fervently wished they could…no, better not revisit that scenario. He was in control again.

She smiled. "That was fun."

"Was it? I didn't notice." He gathered up his clothes and made sure they weren't dripping. "Ready to go inside?"

"If you are." She'd wrapped her clothes into a neat bundle, too.

"What about your boots?"

"I'm leaving them out here for now."

"Then let's go." But he approached her with caution. "If we head straight inside, I'll be fine. If we stand here and blether, I make no promises."

"Blether?" Merriment danced in her eyes. "That sounds naughty."

"It isn't. It's chatting."

"Oh."

"Which is exactly what we're doin', and if we keep it up, I'm liable to forget myself and kiss you."

Her cheeks turned pink. "We'll go in now. I'm in the same fix." She turned away and headed for the door.

"Hearing that doesn't help."

"Maybe hot chocolate will."

"Doubt it."

"Me, too." She opened the door. "Hey, guys, the drowned rats have arrived."

"Come on in." Mandy looked over her shoulder from her spot on the couch facing the fire. A light blanket with teddy bears on it lay over her shoulder and covered her left breast.

Movement under the blanket told him what was going on, even though he was a first timer with this situation.

Mandy confirmed it. "I'm feeding Rhys. Zane's getting the cookies and hot chocolate ready. Are we domestic or what?"

"Who wants whipped cream and who wants marshmallows?" Zane called out from the kitchen.

"I'm a whipped cream girl," Tansy called back. "Can we help?"

"Thanks, but I've got this."

"Whipped cream for me, too, Zane." Aleck glanced at Mandy. "Where should I put my wet clothes for now?"

"On top of the washing machine. Laundry room is right off the kitchen."

"Got it. Hey, Tansy? Want me to take yours, too?"

"I guess. I'll need to remember they're in there, though. I don't want to forget them when I leave."

"I wouldn't count on leaving tonight," Mandy said.

"Sure I can. Piece of cake."

Aleck looked at her. "That road's treacherous."

"Just a little muddy."

"But it's about to get a lot worse." Zane came in with a platter loaded with chocolate chip cookies and a stack of four small plates. "I had the weather channel on a little while ago and the storm's predicted to last into the morning."

"Then maybe I should take off now."

"Please don't, lass."

"I'm with Aleck." Zane set the cookie platter and the plates in the middle of the coffee table. "I've already texted Cody and Rory. They've arranged to stay in town tonight."

"At the B&B?"

"Probably not. Nicole and Bryce have room and so do Ryker and April. When we get a lot of rain, that road can turn into quicksand. And if someone gets stuck, I'll have to go out and get 'em." He gazed at Tansy. "I'm needed here."

"Yeah, okay. You make an excellent point."

Aleck sighed in relief. "Thank the Lord."

"I can just sleep on the couch, though. I don't want to put you guys to any trouble."

Zane smiled. "It's no big deal. This is a four-bedroom house and only two of them are occupied. Take your pick of one of the others and I'll find you a set of sheets."

"In that case, I definitely want the room with the best view."

Mandy laughed. "Sorry, but Kendra gave it to Aleck. He has Cody's old room. It looks out on the chicken coop."

"And you can't beat a chicken-coop view," Zane said. "We charge a premium for it."

"I haven't slept there yet," Aleck said. "I can switch with you."

"I was teasing. It's for one night. I'll take whatever. "

"Then put her in Bryce and Trevor's room," Mandy said. "It's closer to the hall bathroom. She'll have a better chance of beating Aleck in there."

"It's not a competition. I'll let her go first."

"Oh, Aleck," Mandy shook her head. "It most certainly is a competition. Picture the glory days of the bathroom wars, when five teenage boys fought for occupancy. You and Tansy will be carrying on a noble tradition."

He looked at Zane. "Is she makin' that up?"

"Nope, but she's leaving out another time-honored tradition—ladies first."

"I'll go with that one, then."

"Good choice." Zane glanced toward the fireplace. "Tansy, if you'll poke up the fire, Aleck and I will take those clothes to the laundry room and serve up the hot chocolate."

Mandy smiled. "Thanks, my love."

"My pleasure." He walked over, leaned down and gave her a quick kiss. Then he placed another gentle kiss on the blanket, right about where the wee one's head likely was.

Aleck's chest warmed. Having a bairn together looked more appealing tonight than it had this afternoon when Mandy was going through labor. Rory might be onto something.

He followed Zane into the kitchen, made a detour to the laundry room and came out as Zane was pouring the hot chocolate into four mugs. "Does your bairn get enough air under that blanket?"

"Mandy makes sure he does."

"Is the blanket to keep him warm, then?"

"Not in this weather, and especially since I built a fire. The blanket's for modesty's sake. If you guys weren't here she wouldn't bother with it."

"Ah. I don't know much about any of this, but since Rory's set on makin' me an uncle in the next couple of years, I need to learn."

"Rory told me they had a long-range plan. That's exciting."

"It is, but I'm still gettin' used to the idea. He's my younger brother. Can't picture him as a father."

"I can. He'll be a great one. You should see how he acts around Licorice's foal, Eclipse."

"Aye, right. He wants me to meet that wee horse. Maybe tomorrow."

"I'm sure that can be arranged." He rinsed out the hot chocolate pan and put it in the dishwasher. Then he pulled a container out of the refrigerator and opened the lid. "Want to put the whipped cream on?"

"Sure. Is that the real stuff?"

"It is. I was in luck that Mom had some made. I didn't have time to do it myself." He got a spoon out of a drawer.

"Could you?"

"Yeah, it's easy."

"If you say so." He picked up the container and spooned a dollop of whipped cream into each mug. "Never tried it. Rory learned to cook, but I never did. Kind of wish I had, now."

"We didn't have a choice. Mom insisted we all learn how to cook a simple meal, clean a house and operate a washing machine."

Aleck nodded. "Sounds about right. Your ma is somethin' of a legend in our family. My folks marvel at how she raised five boys on her own."

"She's a legend in our family, too." Zane said it without smiling. "I only hope I'll be half as good a parent as she's been."

Aleck met his gaze. "I wouldna worry about that. That wee bairn is lucky to have you."

"Thanks, buddy." He took a breath. "It's an incredible experience. I'm still absorbing the impact of it." Then he glanced at the mugs sitting on the counter. "Better get those delivered before the whipped cream melts." He picked up two mugs and headed out of the kitchen.

Aleck took the other two mugs and followed him into the living room. Tansy had built up the fire and it crackled merrily away as she sat in a chair near the couch talking to Mandy in low tones. Likely they were murmuring so they wouldn't disturb the bairn, who was now on Mandy's other side.

Tansy leaned closer, her gaze on the invisible bairn nursing under the blanket. The tenderness in her expression made him smile. Emotion flowed easily in this town and in this family.

What was it Rory had said today? You feel the current movin' around you. Makes you eager to dive in and be part of it.

Aye, it certainly did.

<u>**12**</u>

By now Tansy thought for sure she'd have kissed Aleck. Instead she wasn't even in kissing distance, let alone free to indulge. He'd taken the chair at the opposite end of the couch and Zane sat next to Mandy and the baby.

The little guy had finished nursing and lay on his tummy, fast asleep and securely wedged between his mom and dad, on his teddy bear blankie.

Since kissing Aleck wasn't an option, she focused on the baby. "So it's Rhys, is it?"

Mandy grinned. "Probably."

"Probably? I heard you call him Rhys when we first arrived."

"It's down to Rhys or Teague. We decided to call him Rhys for a couple of hours and then switch to Teague and see which one resonated. I'd been practicing the name Rhys before you got here and it just came out."

"Huh." Aleck rested his mug on his knee. "And here I thought you'd be exhausted. Instead you're wide awake and testin' names."

"All three of us had a nap after dinner." Zane took a swig of his hot chocolate. "But since then, we've been too excited to sleep. We'll pay for that tomorrow, but right now everything's new and shiny."

"I get it," Tansy said. "The adrenaline's still pumping. Teague's nice."

Mandy looked at Zane. "It is, but...I'm not sure it's right for him."

"Me, either. I know we said we'd switch off, but I like the way you say Rhys."

"I like the way you say it, too. Besides, it has the perfect meaning."

"What is it?" Tansy grabbed another cookie.

Mandy gazed down at the baby. "It's not so obvious now when he's fast asleep, but remember when Ryker said he was so eager to get here that he rushed the gate?"

"I remember that," Aleck said. "Great description."

"That's when I decided it would probably be Rhys." Mandy stroked the baby's back. "It's Celtic and it means enthusiastic."

"Teague's a Celtic name, too," Zane said. "It means handsome poet."

"He'll definitely be handsome," Mandy smoothed his shock of dark hair. "He may or may not be a poet. We already know he's enthusiastic, though." She gazed at Zane. "Have we made our choice, then?"

"We have."

"Wow, and we're part of that special moment." Tansy lifted her mug. "Here's to Rhys McGavin."

"Rhys Ian McGavin. To honor my dad."

"Well done," Aleck said. "My da will like knowing that. And my gran and grandpa, too."

"Then here's to Rhys Ian McGavin." Tansy lifted her mug a second time. "May he continue to live enthusiastically."

"Aye." Aleck raised his mug in the baby's direction. "Enthusiasm is a very good thing."

Mandy and Zane touched mugs and smiled. They'd clearly reached the stage in their relationship where words were unnecessary.

Tansy admired the heck out of that. "Since you didn't expect to have kibitzers during this process, we can keep this to ourselves until you're ready to make a big announcement."

"Aye, we can." Aleck reached for another cookie. "Our lips are sealed."

Speaking of lips, he had sexy ones, firm on the top and sensual on the bottom. No telling when she'd get a chance to find out if they felt as good as they looked, though.

"I've been thinking about how to do the name reveal." Zane took a swig of his hot chocolate. "It's not like we have a planned gathering tomorrow where we could create some drama. What's your take on it, Mandy?"

"I say we write a cheerful text and send it to everyone."

"When?"

"Might as well do it now. Some are still up, and the ones who've gone to bed will see it first thing in the morning." She picked up her phone from the coffee table. "Sending something in writing has the added benefit of letting everyone know how we're spelling it R-H-Y-S."

"That was my guess," Aleck said. "Then again, I'm from that part of the world. Will everyone know how to pronounce it?"

"I think so." She started typing. "But I'll say it sounds like *Reese* so there's no question."

"It's a great name. He'll fit right in with all the other enthusiastic McGavins." Tansy glanced at Aleck. "You should have seen Aleck arm-wrestling Ryker before—"

"Wait. He did what?" Zane stared at her before turning to Aleck. "I can't believe Ryker would suggest such a thing."

"He didn't." Aleck stood and picked up his mug and plate. "I challenged him."

Zane sighed. "I doubt that was a lot of fun for you."

"Aye, it was fun. We ended in a stalemate."

"What?"

"It's true," Tansy said.

"That never happens."

"It did tonight."

"Incredible. You must be a hell of an arm-wrestler, Aleck."

"I do all right."

"Don't forget he was jetlagged," Mandy said. "Sounds like if he'd been rested he would have won the match."

"Nay, I wouldn't go that far. But now that I'm on my feet, I'll admit I'm ready to call it a night."

Tansy stood. "Me, too." She glanced at Zane. "Did you say something about sheets?"

"Sure did. I'll fetch them." He got up from the couch.

"I'll come with you. And for the record, I'm honored that I could be here for the official naming moment." Tansy's gaze encompassed the adorable new family. "It's been a special treat."

"For me, too." Aleck came over to collect her dishes. "I'll take these and put them in the dishwasher."

"Thanks for that." She turned to Zane. "Lead the way." She followed him down the hall.

He gestured to the first room on the right. "That's where Aleck's staying."

"The room with the chicken-coop view."

"Exactly. I imagine you already know where the bathroom is."

"Found it today during the festivities."

"Your room is right across from it."

And next to Aleck's. Not that it made any difference. No secret rendezvous would take place tonight.

Zane walked past the bathroom and opened a bi-fold door just beyond it. "Linen closet."

"Just toss the sheets in my direction. I can make my own bed."

"It's not as easy as it sounds." He handed her sheets and a pillowcase. "It's a bunk bed."

"Unless you're going to grade me on neatness, I'll be fine. Like I said, it's one night."

"Guess so. Blankets are already in there. Here's a bath towel and a washcloth." After adding them to the pile in her arms, he glanced toward the ceiling. "Still coming down. Thanks for not giving me an argument about staying."

"I saw the light. By the way, how's this weather affecting Raptors Rise?"

He closed the bi-fold door. "The sanctuary's covered. I brought in extra personnel in anticipation of the baby, and now that our road's paved, they can get in and out."

"That's good."

He glanced at her. "The match with Ryker was really a stalemate?"

"Scouts honor." She gave him a brief description that had him shaking his head. "No telling how long it would have gone on if Bryce hadn't asked them to call it a draw."

"Ryker would have won it eventually."

"I wouldn't be too sure. Aleck—"

"I would have lost that match." He appeared at the end of the hall and walked toward them. "That's what you're talkin' about, right?"

"Zane wanted more detail."

"Bryce saved my bacon by intervenin'. Another minute and I would have gone down in flames. That's why I should give Ryker a rematch."

Zane grinned. "No, you shouldn't. A small dose of humility won't hurt my brother at all."

"And Rory was so proud of you," Tansy said. "Did you see his face?"

"Aye. Sometimes he overestimates my abilities, though. I swear he thinks I can do anythin'."

"Of course he does." Zane shoved his hands in his pockets. "I think that about Ryker. If you'd beat him, I would be all for a rematch because I'd know how much he needed one. But a draw? That's only a small blow to his ego. I hope you let it lay."

"I'll think about it."

"Okay." Zane extended his hand. "Glad you could be here today, Aleck. The bagpipe lullaby meant a lot to me. Brought my dad closer."

"I'm glad." He gripped Zane's hand. "Meant a lot to me, too."

"I'll leave you two to work out the bathroom schedule. Tansy, help yourself to anything you need. Mom keeps all sorts of toiletries in there for situations like this one."

"Do you have unexpected company a lot?"

"More than you might think. Make yourself at home. I'll go see how Mandy and Rhys are doing."

"Thanks, Zane," she called after him. Then she glanced at Aleck. "Such a good guy."

"They all are."

"That's for sure. Tell you what. I'll go dump these sheets and then take my turn in the bathroom. I'll make the bed afterward. That way I won't hold you up."

"I don't mind."

"Because you're a good guy, too." She flashed him a smile before hurrying into the room she'd been assigned. Standing around *blethering* only made her want to kiss him. Making out in the hall when Zane or Mandy could show up anytime wasn't the venue she preferred.

She flipped the wall switch and a lamp on the dresser came on. The base was a model of a covered wagon, the sort of thing two young cowboys in training would think was cool.

Tossing the sheets on the lower bunk, she grabbed the washcloth and towel before going across the hall to the bathroom. Aleck had left his door open and rustling noises indicated he was unpacking. Probably the first chance he'd had.

She took Zane at his word and rummaged around in the vanity. She found a new toothbrush still in its package and a tube of toothpaste. After using those, she washed her face and finger-combed her hair. Some lotion from a pump dispenser on the counter and she was good to go.

When she came out, Mandy and Zane's laughter drifted from the living room. Judging from bits and pieces of their conversation, they'd received plenty of texted comments on the name choice. The McGavin clan wasn't shy about stating an opinion.

She walked into her bedroom and stopped short.

Aleck's back was turned as he put the finishing touches on her bed. "Thought I'd make myself useful."

"Thank you." Her heart beat a rapid tattoo. She hadn't expected to encounter him again tonight, yet here he was, very much in her space. Bold move.

He turned. "This evenin' didn't end quite like I expected."

She took a shaky breath. "Not like I expected, either."

"I counted on Zane and Mandy bein'—"

"Asleep. Seemed logical they would be." In this small room he seemed taller and more imposing than he had when they were all sitting by the fire.

"I'm not complainin', though." He moved a step closer. "Because of them, you're here instead of out in the storm. I was determined to stop you from drivin' that road tonight, but I couldn't figure out how."

"I see now it would have been a dumb move."

"Not dumb." He moved close enough to cup her face in his hand. "Headstrong, maybe." Heat flickered in his green eyes. "Not such a bad thing." He brushed his thumb over her cheek.

She couldn't seem to breathe properly. "I…could have caused a lot of trouble."

"But you saw reason. You stayed. And I get a chance to steal a wee goodnight kiss." He lowered his head.

Trembling with anticipation, she closed her eyes. "Only a wee kiss?"

His sexy chuckle hinted at intimacies yet to come. "Might be a bit more than that." And he touched down.

13

At last. Surely Aleck had waited days for this moment, not mere hours. Gently, gently... learning the shape of Tansy's mouth, the perfect bow, the lush fullness...wanting...more. Dizzy. Breathless. *Alive.*

Cupping her face in both hands, he shifted the angle, took the kiss deeper, tasted eagerness on her tongue. Sparks...heat...longing...

She fisted her hands in his t-shirt. Moaned. Rose on tiptoe, clutched the back of his head.

Ahhh. Holding her, winding himself around her warmth, gathering her in...breathing her in...aching...

Gasping, she spun away.

He stared at her through a red haze, chest heaving, gulping for air. "Tansy..." A tortured plea wrapped in her name.

She pressed a hand to her chest and swallowed. "I...have to...stop."

He closed his eyes and dragged in a breath. "Aye." Another breath, and another. Then he trusted himself to look at her. Even so, he took an involuntary step forward.

Flushed cheeks, bright eyes, rosy mouth damp from his kiss...how was he to walk out of this room?

"I think—" She paused to clear her throat. "I was about to take advantage of you."

A burst of cooling laughter did the trick. The driving need to hold her eased a wee bit. "I believe it was the other way 'round, lass."

"Believe what you want." She sucked in more air. "Another few seconds and I would have had you under my spell."

"You already do."

She held his gaze. "We have a situation."

"Aye." He blew out a breath. "A highly flammable one."

"Did you suspect?"

He nodded.

"Me, too. But it's more than I..." She touched her mouth. "You'd better go."

"I would if I could."

"What's stopping you?"

He shrugged. "My feet are nailed to the floor."

"Now that's a problem."

"Any ideas?"

"Hundreds. You?"

"Thousands. All impossible under the circumstances."

"Hey, guys!" Zane's voice signaled his approach.

"That works." He turned to face the open door. "Hey, Zane. We're in Tansy's room."

His cousin appeared in the doorway looking confused. "Everything okay?"

"Uh…sure…we were just…"

"Everything's just fine!" Tansy's chipper reply came off fake as hell, but better than his non-response.

"Good. That's good. I see you got the bed made. Bunks are tough. Neat job."

"Thanks." Aleck said it out of habit. "I mean—"

"He was generous enough to make it while I was in the bathroom." Tansy still sounded like she was high on something.

"Considerate of you, cuz." Zane gave him a questioning glance, as well he might. Everyone else in the family had figured out an attraction was brewing. But he'd been so involved with his wife and his bairn that he was out of the loop.

Aleck shoved his hands in his pockets. "I try."

"Yeah, well, Mandy sent me to tell both of you that breakfast will be catch-as-catch-can. We can't guarantee we'll be in the kitchen frying up eggs and making coffee in the morning, so you're welcome to commandeer the facilities and fix yourself whatever you want."

"Don't worry about us," Tansy said. "Let us know if there's anything we can do for you guys."

Zane smiled. "That's a nice offer. We'll see how it goes. I'll be up early in any case. Gotta feed those critters."

"Oh, my gosh, that's right! If the road's out it'll only be you. I'll help."

"That's okay. You don't have to. The work load's not too bad. Several of our boarders are off on holiday rides elsewhere. I can handle—"

"No, I'll definitely help. I've never been here at feeding time, but I used to pitch in when I was riding at the stable back in Boston. Can't be terribly different."

"I know absolutely nothing about feedin' horses," Aleck said, "but surely I can be of some use."

"Thanks, Aleck, but Rory mentioned that you're not into this kind of thing. I wouldn't want to—"

"By all means, put me to work. There's no way I'll sit up here drinkin' coffee while you and Tansy are slavin' away in the barn."

"Alrighty, then. The horses will appreciate it and so will I."

"Only thing I'm worried about is gettin' my boots dirty."

Zane ducked his head but didn't quite manage to hide his grin. When he looked up, only a flash of humor in his eyes gave him away. "I can fix that problem."

"I'd appreciate it."

"We should have some rubber boots around here. Might even be in this bedroom closet. Let's look." Moving into the room, he opened a door. "Yep, just as I thought." He picked up a pair of brown rain boots and handed them over. "These should fit. Rubber is more forgiving than leather."

"I'm sure they'll be fine. What time do you feed the horses?"

"Sunup."

"When's that?"

"About five-thirty."

He swallowed a groan. "I'll be there. See you both in the mornin'." He walked out of the room.

"Have a good night," Tansy called after him.

"You, too, lass!" He went into his room, shut the door and leaned against it. Rain pounded on the roof, energetic as his brother's sticks on the snare drum.

He'd agreed to meet Zane down at the barn at sunup. Might not be any sun. Might still be raining. Quite likely mud would be involved. He'd be feeding large animals he knew nothing about and likely dealing with their poop.

So what? Tansy would be there. For a chance to spend time with her, he'd clean out stalls with his bare hands.

* * *

Aleck's phone alarm chimed at five. Two other sounds registered—rain on the roof and loud clucking. He peered into the semi-darkness outside his window and sure enough, Zane was moving around the chicken coop, scattering seed in the rain. Rural life. Bloody tough, in his estimation.

Pulling on his jeans, he went to the door and opened it a crack. A light shone under the bathroom door and the shower was going. Really?

She was showering before she hiked down to the barn through rain and mud?

He ran his hand over his bristle. On the other hand, a quick shower would feel great and he should also shave. Walking back to the dresser, he grabbed his shaving kit. Then he opened his door and leaned against the jam, chest tight with anticipation as he waited for her to come out.

He'd dreamed about her, dreams involving porches, stripping down and making love in the rain. Better not dwell on that. Greeting her with a bulge in his pants was not classy.

The doorknob turned and he held his breath. She came out wrapped in a pink towel that matched the streaks in her wet hair. She kept the towel secure with one hand and carried a hair dryer in the other.

"Oh!" She stopped abruptly. "Good morning." Her gaze traveled over his bare chest and her tempting mouth curved in a smile.

Evidently he'd passed inspection. He pushed away from the doorframe. "Good—" The word came out as a croak. She was just that lovely. He cleared his throat. "Good mornin' to you, too, lass." Only a towel and a few feet of hallway separated him from all he'd dreamed of during the night.

He couldn't have more than a kiss, though. They had a schedule to keep. But a kiss was better than nothing. He could almost taste it as he took a step toward her.

Then Mandy came out of the master bedroom with Rhys in her arms. "Hey, guys! Looks like everybody's up! Zane said you'd offered to help feed and I'm so grateful."

He caught the flash of amusement in Tansy's eyes. She'd likely read his intent loud and clear. "He's gettin' a numptie with me," he said, "but I'll give it my best."

"With Tansy and Zane to guide you, you'll be fine." Mandy glanced down at the impossibly tiny bairn. "Won't they, Rhys?"

The wee babe was more pink than red this morning. He gazed up at his mother intently, his brow wrinkled.

"He looks worried," Aleck said. "I think he knows an amateur when he sees one."

Mandy laughed. "I'm sure he's figured out I am, poor kid. I'm all thumbs with the diaper routine. I keep waiting for that instinctive tribal knowledge to kick in, but so far, it's like any other first day on the job. I suck."

"I doubt it." Tansy moved closer to Mandy. "He looks good. Did you guys have a peaceful night?"

Mandy smiled. "We did, although we didn't sleep much. Kept admiring this little guy. How about you two?"

"I can't speak for Aleck, but I was asleep the minute my head hit the pillow."

"Same here. Slept like a log." And woke up with a woody.

"I need to get out of your way so you can get dressed and go help Zane." Mandy continued down the hall. "He's out there feeding the chickens, poor guy."

"Saw that," Aleck called after her.

"Rub it in." Tansy gave him a saucy glance. "Lord it over those of us who don't have a chicken-coop view."

"That I will, and it's worth every penny."

"Do you need this?" She held up the dryer. "If so, I can—"

"Don't need it. I'll just shower and shave, skip the hair for now."

"Then the bathroom's all yours." She gestured with the hair dryer.

"Thanks." He quickly estimated whether he dared kiss her. Nope. Too much time had passed. Could sabotage the entire plan. "See you in a few." He started toward the bathroom.

"I hope you're not shaving for me."

"Why?" Because he was.

"I think you look hot with a little scruff."

"Then I'll just wash up a bit." He walked into the bathroom and closed the door. "She thinks I look hot with a little scruff," he informed his reflection. "Let's hope those ugly rubber boots don't cancel out my hotness factor."

Eliminating his shave meant he was showered, dressed and ready to go before she was. He'd brought a rain jacket with a hood so he put that on before tapping on her door. Wasn't risking his Stetson again. "I'll wait for you in the livin' room."

"You can go down ahead of me if you want."

"I'd rather not. I'm hopin' for pointers on the way there. I'll wait for you."

"Truly, it's not that hard."

"Easy for you to say. How long have you been ridin'?"

"Since I was nine."

"That puts you kilometers ahead of me. I don't know one end of a horse from the other."

"The front end eats the hay and the back end—"

"Just kiddin'."

"Me, too." She opened her door and came out wearing a Guzzling Grizzly hooded sweatshirt, jeans and her boots, which had been cleaned.

"Look at you, lass! When did you have time to scrape the mud off your boots?"

"Zane did it. They washed our stuff, too, but your jeans are still in the dryer. Guess they're thicker denim than mine. Mandy loaned me a sweatshirt."

"I don't know how those two are still upright, let alone doin' laundry."

"They're high on the joys of parenthood. Ready to go?"

"Ready as I'll ever be."

"One more thing." Bracing her hand on his shoulder, she lifted to her toes and gave him a quick but potent kiss.

He groaned. "Damn, lass. That makes me want—"

"Later." She patted his chest. "Trust me, we'll find time." She started down the hall.

As he followed her, he continued to process her unexpected kiss. His lips tingled and his pulse hammered. "I hope you mean that, because I'm goin' crazy."

"My shift at the GG begins at six tonight. That gives us plenty of hours to work with."

"Rory wants to get in some practice time on our numbers for the parade."

"That's important. We'll work around any obligations."

"I wish I didn't have to leave on Friday, but I'm expected back."

"I understand." She turned to him as they reached the front door. "We'll make every moment count."

"Aye." He took a deep breath. "We will."

She opened the door and walked out on the porch. "Still raining."

"Yep."

"I could ask Mandy if she has an umbrella we could use."

"I haven't been here long, but that doesn't sound like how a McGavin operates."

"You've got that right. They laugh at the rain. And the snow, the sleet and the hail."

He held out his hand. "Then let's make a run for it."

"Didn't you want pointers along the way? You won't get any if we're racing in the rain."

"Who needs pointers?" He flashed her a grin. "I'm a McGavin. It's in my blood."

<u>*14*</u>

Aleck's manly scruff and rakish smile were a lethal combo. Even the ugly rain boots couldn't make a dent in his sexy Scottish appeal. He should have had trouble running in them, but he was amazingly agile in those things. Halfway to the barn he let out a *yee-haw* that made Tansy laugh so hard she almost couldn't run at all.

Light from inside the barn cut through the gray drizzle, giving them a target. Zane had left the sliding barn door open wide enough for them to fit through one at a time.

Aleck skidded to a stop at the entrance, raindrops clinging to his eyelashes and scruff. The barn provided a windbreak. "You first," he said, panting.

"What was that *yee-haw* all about?"

"Only cowboy phrase I know. Seemed like the time to use it."

"Yeah." She grinned. "Guess it was." Resisting the urge to kiss him again, she ducked inside. He was quickly becoming irresistible.

A wheelbarrow full of fragrant hay stood in front of her. Zane wheeled a similarly loaded one down the wooden aisle toward the back of the barn. Winston, a butterscotch and white Paint in the last stall on the right, trumpeted a greeting. Horses' noses poked out from the other stalls as Zane passed by with the wheelbarrow.

"We're here," Tansy called out. "Want us to close the barn door?"

"You can leave it," he said over his shoulder. "The rain's coming from the other direction and the horses love a little fresh air. If you two will follow me down to the end, I'll get you started."

"On our way." She flipped back her hood and turned to check on Aleck.

He stood with his hands shoved in his back pockets and his hood thrown back as he made a visual sweep of the barn. He met her gaze. "Just needed a minute to take it all in. Let's go."

She started off. "You've never been in a barn?"

"Not one as grand as this." He fell into step beside her. "Gran and Grandpa have a sheep barn, but it doesn't compare."

"The new one is more utilitarian, but I love this one more. It's elegant."

"Good word for it." He eyed the horses keeping track of their progress. "Do you think they can sense I'm a numptie?"

"Not unless you're afraid of them. Are you?"

He shook his head. "Cautious. Curious. And to my surprise, fascinated."

"All good things when you're dealing with horses."

Zane turned the wheelbarrow around and lowered the handles before coming out from behind it to greet them. "Thanks for doing this, guys."

"You're most welcome," Tansy said. "How're you holding up, family man? Heard you were up with the chickens and out with 'em, too."

He gave them a weary smile. "The adrenaline rush is wearing off. Talked to Mom this morning and she was glad you'd volunteered. They're pinned down, too. Even Quinn's road is washed out and his property is higher than ours."

"I'm glad we're here to help." Aleck surveyed the two rows of stalls. "Plenty of horses to feed."

"Normally I can handle it, but like I was telling Winston, I—"

"Who's Winston?" Aleck glanced around as if expecting a person to show up.

"Right over there." Tansy pointed to the gelding. "Hey, Winston! How're you doin', boy?"

He whinnied in response.

Made her laugh. "If you talk to him, he talks back."

"No kiddin'?"

"It's the truth," Zane said. "He's a good listener, too. Winston and I have had some long discussions."

"Interestin' name for a horse. The only Winston I've heard of is Churchill."

"That's who we named him for," Zane said. "Both big talkers."

Aleck grinned. "I like that."

Winston snorted and bobbed his head. Then he made a low-throated noise that sounded like grumbling.

"Now he's telling us he's starving and we need to get a move on." Zane handed over two pairs of work gloves.

"Thanks." Tansy pulled hers on. "And thank you for cleaning the mud off my boots. That was above and beyond. I'm afraid they're messed up again."

"No worries. At least it's fresh mud." He grabbed a bundle of hay. "A hay flake goes in the hay net in each stall. Like this." He opened Winston's stall and demonstrated. Then he gave Winston a pat on the rump as he left the stall. "The pat is optional."

"Very much like what I'm used to." Tansy glanced at Aleck. "You good to go?"

"Aye. I'll follow your lead."

Zane gestured toward a dappled gray who was wearing his typical hangdog expression. "Aleck, you can start with Eeyore. He's Mandy's horse."

"Looks a wee bit peely-wally to me."

"He's fine. He does his best to appear pathetic so people will feel sorry for him. He's been pulling that for years, even though we treat him like royalty."

"And so will I." Aleck picked up a hay flake. "Cheer up, laddie. I'm here to serve your highness."

"I'll start with Bert and Ernie." Tansy turned to the right and opened Bert's stall.

"Bert and Ernie." Aleck chuckled. "I'm gettin' a kick out of these names. Must be fun thinkin' them up."

"Yeah, it is." Zane didn't quite smother his yawn.

"I heard that yawn." Tansy came out of Bert's stall and closed the door. "You're dead on your feet, aren't you?"

"I'm okay."

"Uh-huh. You'd say that if you were ready to pass out."

Aleck come out of Eeyore's stall. "I think I have the hang of this routine. I gave him a pat but couldn't tell if he liked it or not."

Zane chuckled. "He did but he won't show it." He rolled his shoulders. "Carry on. I'll start at the other end and meet you in the middle."

"I have a better idea," Tansy said. "Going by what you said last night, there are fewer horses in the other barn."

"That's true. Once we finish with this bunch, we'll have the bulk of it done."

"Then let us handle the horses in this barn while you take care of the ones over there."

"That's not fair. I'll finish way before you."

"That's the point. When you're done, you can go back to the house and sleep."

"While you're still working? I couldn't do that."

"Sure you could."

"What if you run into a problem?"

She pulled out her phone. "We won't, but on the small chance that we suddenly need you down here, I'll call."

He rubbed the back of his neck and stared into space. Then he let out a long sigh. "I'll consider it. I'll head over to the other barn and come back this way when I'm done to see how you're faring." He clamped a battered cowboy hat on his head. "Thanks, guys." He zipped his jacket and left the barn.

Aleck gazed after him. "He's lookin' a bit peely-wally, too."

"Peely-wally." She grinned. "Great description. And yes, he's clearly exhausted. He needs to let us do this so he can crash."

"Then let's get to it. Who's this next one I'm deliverin' to?"

"That's either Bonnie or Clyde. They look a lot alike." She carried a flake of hay into Ernie's stall. "This pair's easy. Bert's the taller one and Ernie's the shorter, stockier one. Bonnie and Clyde are almost identical."

"There's one sure way to tell which is which."

"That's—"

"Obvious, right? Which is likely why you didn't think of it. I'll check it out and let you know."

"Okay, you do that." This would be fun.

He delivered a flake to the first horse and came out of the stall. "That one is definitely Clyde."

"If you say so."

"I know so. He has a tadger. He seems to be missing the rest of his equipment, though."

"Because he's a gelding." She smiled at his use of the word *tadger*. Thanks to Damaris, she knew what the Scottish word meant.

"Does that mean he's been neutered?"

"Yes. Stallions usually aren't a good choice for a riding stable. Geldings are more reliable."

"That's logical. Even I can see that you wouldn't want a hot-blooded stallion out on a trail ride. Could create a legal liability."

"Definitely." She moved down the line. "This is Diablo, the horse Rory's been riding ever since he came to the ranch."

"He told me about Diablo. He looks too calm to have that name, though."

"He was already named when Kendra got him."

"Maybe he was a right chancer of a stallion."

"That would explain it, but he's extremely safe now. He'd be a good choice for you when we go out today."

"Ridin'?"

"Sure."

"In this?"

"It might let up."

"Aye, but if the road's so muddy that nobody's comin' or goin', surely that's not ridin' weather."

"Horses can go where trucks can't. They can take the high road, so to speak."

"That may be, but I still don't think—"

"You wouldn't be trying to avoid that ride, would you?"

"Not at all. I just..." He met her gaze. "Aye. That's what I'm doin'. I could land on my bum under the best of circumstances. Add in a rain-slicked saddle and I'll fly off straight away."

"Would you feel better if we wait for the sun to come out?"

"I would."

"Then we will." Clearly his manly pride was at stake and he didn't relish taking a tumble in front of her. She got that. "Just remember you're an athletic guy. I have no doubt you'll be good at this."

"Aye, right." He picked up another hay flake. "Time to feed Bonnie."

"Are you sure that's Bonnie?" She gave him another chance to reconsider his assumption.

"No other option."

"Okay." She brought Diablo his hay and waited for the inevitable discovery.

"Here you go, Bonnie." Aleck's voice drifted across the aisle. "Got some hay for you, lass. I..." A moment of silence. "Tansy, somethin's not right."

"Oh?" She turned toward him and controlled the urge to giggle. "What do you mean?"

"Bonnie has a tadger."

"I know." She cleared the laughter from her throat.

He looked thoroughly confused. "Who would name two geldings *Bonnie and Clyde*?"

"Olivia."

"The same Olivia who's with Trevor?"

"Yes. She always wanted a matched set of bays and she decided in advance to name them Bonnie and Clyde. When she ended up with two geldings, she used the names, anyway."

"Huh." He turned back to study the horses. "No wonder you can't tell 'em apart. My apologies for thinkin' you'd missed the obvious."

"Apology accepted."

He gave her a sheepish grin. "I made a right fool of myself, didn't I?"

"It was an easy mistake to make."

"Especially if you're feeling out of your depth and trying to show off your powers of deduction like some Scottish arse I'm acquainted with. Well played, lass."

"Thanks."

"Are all of them geldings, then?"

"All except Licorice and Eclipse."

He brightened. "Eclipse! I forgot about that wee horse. Where is he?"

"Over here with his mom. They're my next delivery."

"I'm amazed I didn't think of them when I first came in here. I want to see." He crossed the aisle and peered into the stall. "Look at that." He said it quietly, as if he didn't want to disturb the nursing colt. "He's gettin' his breakfast. And Licorice is just standin' there bein' patient."

"She's turned out to be a good mom, even though prior to this she's been a challenge."

"She seems mellow enough, now." He rested his forearms on the stall door. "It's an interestin' contrast, with her so black and sleek and him so fluffy and brown."

"He's a cutie, for sure. Ah, he's done nursing. Now you'll get a better view of his face."

As if knowing he was being admired, the colt turned, showing off the distinctive white crescent on his forehead.

"It sure does look like the sun peekin' out from behind the Earth's shadow. Hey, he's comin' over."

The colt took a few tentative steps in their direction. Then Licorice nickered, and he returned to her side.

"She called him back, didn't she?" He sounded disappointed.

"She's being protective because she doesn't know you. When Rory gets here, I'm sure he'll take you out in the pasture with them. That's always fun."

"I'd like that. Rory thinks it's pure barry that he got to name this wee horse."

"Pure barry must be good."

"Very good. Fantastic." He shifted his weight and his shoulder brushed hers. "He thought we'd have time yesterday to come to the barn and see him, but that didn't work out."

The shoulder brush was probably an accident. Her body reacted, anyway. "It's been quite a jam-packed schedule ever since you arrived."

"Fun, though."

"Pure barry?"

"Aye." A telltale huskiness in his voice gave him away.

She turned her head and sure enough, he'd switched his attention from the colt to her. She swallowed. "I'm glad you're having a good time."

"Oh, I am, lass." He held her gaze with those smiling green eyes. "Any chance you had a secondary reason for sending Zane off?"

"I might've."

"Then we'd best finish the job." He pushed away from the stall door and glanced at the wheelbarrow. "We're almost out of flakes. I'll get the other lot from the front."

"Okay. Thanks." As he walked away, she admired the determined set of his broad shoulders and the shift of muscles in his tight buns. *Only three days.* Asking for something that would inconvenience strangers wasn't nice, but that didn't stop her from wishing for his flight to be cancelled.

15

A gelding named Bonnie. Aleck chuckled as he went back to delivering hay flakes. He should have seen it coming. Tansy had sent up a warning signal right away—*if you say so.*

Then when he'd insisted one piece of evidence clinched the deal she'd sent up another flare—*are you sure?* She'd neatly put him in his place. He'd best not be underestimating that lass. She'd keep him on his toes. And that turned him on.

Feeding the horses was more entertaining and informative than he'd anticipated. He enjoyed stroking their silky necks and they seemed to like a little scratch, too. The work was good exercise. After a while he took off his jacket and hung it over the handle of the wheelbarrow. Next time he returned for more hay, Tansy's jacket was on the other handle.

Since their wee break spent admiring Eclipse, they'd worked steadily without talking. Didn't mean he'd forgotten she was there. Just the opposite.

In the silence broken only by the crunch of horses chomping on hay, her footsteps on the wooden floor seemed amplified. When her breathing quickened, the soft inhale and exhale fueled his imagination. After several minutes of that, he was ready to switch from caressing horses to caressing Tansy. Not possible. Yet.

Not long after that, Zane showed up. "I'm done over there." He started down the aisle toward them. "Looks like you're coming along fine."

"Oh, yeah, we're in good shape." Tansy picked up another hay flake. "Go get some sleep, okay?"

"Yeah, but if I helped you, then we could all—"

"Zane, you have to be puggled." Aleck stepped into the aisle and intercepted him. "It's high time for you to relax."

"That's what Mandy said. I just texted her and Rhys is asleep. She's gonna take a nap."

"Then why not join her? Tansy and I will be fine here. She knows what she's doin' and we'll call you if we end up in a guddle."

"I hate to abandon you. Let's finish up so we can all go to the house and grab some breakfast."

Let's not. Aleck lowered his voice. "Please go back without us. We'll be along later."

"Huh?" Zane's brows snapped together. "You must be getting hungry. I'm a fair hand in the kitchen."

"We'll wait on breakfast."

"But—"

"I doubt you've noticed, but while you've been busy welcomin' a bairn..." Aleck dropped his voice to a murmur. "Tansy and I discovered... many things in common."

Zane scrubbed a hand over his face. "Oh." Then he blinked. "*Oh*. Why didn't you say so?"

"Tryin' to be subtle."

"I'm way too tired for subtle." He raised his voice so Tansy could hear him. "Aleck's convinced me. I'll pack it in. We can turn them out after the rain lets up. Come to the house and make yourselves something to eat whenever you're ready."

"We will," Tansy called out. "'Bye, Zane." After he left, she laughed softly. "That was funny."

"What?"

"You told him to scram, didn't you?"

"I was nice about it." He delivered another hay flake and took a quick count of the remaining stalls. "Only four left."

"I'm aware." She reached the wheelbarrow at the same time he did. "I feel like I'm back in high school sneaking off somewhere to make out with a boy." She grabbed another flake and ducked into the next stall.

"Desperate times call for desperate measures." And every time he looked at her he became more desperate.

"I've been thinking about your flight out. Why Friday? Wouldn't Sunday make more sense?"

"It would, but the head of the firm called an emergency meeting for Saturday. One of our biggest clients is threatening to leave and Campbell wants to brainstorm a strategy to keep him."

"So the meeting was a last-minute thing?" She came back for more hay.

"He announced it a week ago. I'd planned to stay longer, but then this came up and I changed my return flight."

"He wouldn't make an exception for a special trip to see family?" She glanced over her shoulder as she continued working.

"Not considering what's on the line. I wasn't the only one who had to change plans."

"You like your job, though, right?"

"Love my job. I'm not fond of Campbell, but this kind of thing doesn't happen often."

"Then I guess you'd better go home on Friday."

"Aye." He walked into the last stall on his side. "What's this horse's name?"

"That's Strawberry. Kendra put me on him for my first ride out here. He's very gentle and she wanted to make sure I wasn't blowing smoke about how much experience I'd had. Now she lets me ride whoever I want, but I've stuck with Strawberry. I'll take him when we go out today."

"Still rainin'." Shedding his gloves, he tossed them in the wheelbarrow.

"Could stop any time."

"But it's so cozy in here with the rain on the roof. Perfect kissin' weather." He walked around it to meet her as she came out of the last stall on her side. "Are we done, lass?"

"Looks like it to me." She pulled off her gloves.

"I'll take those." After she handed them to him, he tossed them over his shoulder.

She grinned and shook her head. "Neither one landed in the wheelbarrow."

"Don't care." Sliding his hands around her waist, he drew her closer. "But now I wish I'd shaved."

Reaching up, she stroked his beard. "And I'm glad you didn't. I like it."

His breath hitched. "So you said."

"You left it for me?" She held his gaze as she traced his eyebrows with the tips of her fingers.

"Aye." That butterfly touch was stealing the oxygen from his lungs. He dragged in a breath. "When a lass says I look hot with a beard, only a bloke with a head full o' mince would shave it."

She continued to explore his face with the tips of her fingers, sliding them over his cheekbones, brushing them across his lower lip. "I'm glad you didn't."

"Even so, I worry about your fair skin." He tucked her against his hips. His tadger loved that. The top of her head barely topped his shoulder, yet somehow her body and his fit perfectly. "Makes me wonder if I'm makin' a mistake, kissin' you right now."

"Well, my head must be full o' mince, because I'm not at all worried about your beard." Her brown eyes grew luminous. "And I do so want you to kiss me, Aleck."

Desire slammed into him. "I want that, too, lass." He cradled her head in one hand and pressed her close with the other. "So much." He leaned down.

She met him halfway, her eyelashes fluttering closed and her lips parting in welcome. At the last moment, he shut his eyes, too, and sank down on the velvet richness of her mouth.

No rushing. He'd savor each new delight as it unfolded under the coaxing movement of his lips and the gentle probe of his tongue. She snuggled closer and the sap began to rise in his eager body.

Easy, easy. He'd never been this quick to catch fire. Could he bank those flames? Aye. He could and he would. Never mind that she'd undressed a few feet away from him only hours before. Delving deeper into her warm mouth was pleasure enough this morning.

Ah, but the temptation of her plump breasts lured him. Her aroused nipples left a subtle imprint as she snuggled close. Drawing away from the kiss, she dragged in a breath.

His groin tightened and he fought the impulses demanding satisfaction, the hunger pushing him to—

"Touch me."

His tadger throbbed. "I canna do more than that."

"I *know.* I just need…"

Heart pounding, he slid his hand under the back of her shirt. Warm skin against his palm nearly destroyed his already shaky control. He unhooked her bra. "This?"

"*Yes.*"

"Ah, Tansy." He found his way beneath her unhooked bra and cupped the tender weight of her breast. "You're tremblin'."

"It's you." She struggled for each breath. "I'm never like this."

"Like what, lass?" Caressing her was costing him. His jeans had become a denim vice squeezing his privates. But he'd suffer gladly for the pleasure of stroking her silken skin.

"Wanting...*craving*...you. Ever since...ever since last night, I—" She paused to drag in air. "I'm obsessed with your mouth. It's insane."

"I'm honored." He brushed his lips over hers.

"More, please."

"Gladly." He took possession again, shifting the angle to go deeper. He gave that kiss all he had.

She moaned low in her throat and arched her back, pushing her breast against the rhythmic flex of his fingers. The longer he kissed her, the more he ached. His tadger was in big trouble. When she sucked on his tongue, he almost came.

With another heartfelt groan, she slowly drew away, clearly struggling to gain a bit of control. When she'd put a couple of millimeters between her mouth and his, she paused, breathing hard.

He was in the same shape. He was prideful regarding his lung capacity, developed over years of playing the pipes. But his legendary lungs couldn't stand up to a hot session of kissing Tansy.

"I'm dizzy," she murmured.

"Me, too."

"If we..." She took several more breaths. "If we were horizontal..."

"Wouldn't help."

"It would."

"You can't breathe better lyin' down."

"But you can do other things besides kiss."

"Is that so?" He'd laugh if he had the breath to do it. "What things?"

"The ones that require a condom."

"Bold talk." He nibbled on her lower lip.

"We need to bring it up."

"Believe me, it's up."

"You're a funny guy."

"And you're the most excitin' woman I've ever had the pleasure of kissin'. Standin' up or lyin' down."

"I'd like to try this lying down."

"I like that plan." He placed wee kisses over every millimeter of her face. "But I don't fancy implementin' it here at the ranch house."

"Me, either. We need to go to my apartment."

"Can't get there now. The road." He combed back her hair and trailed kisses down the curve of her neck.

"I know." Closing her eyes, she relaxed against him. "I just..." She moaned softly and her breath quickened. "That feels so good. I can only imagine how good it would feel..."

"Everywhere?" He nuzzled behind her ear. He should stop kissing her. Although his mouth loved doing it, his tadger and his baws were in serious pain. Just a wee bit longer and he'd—

Her cell phone rang. "*Shoot.*"

Much as he didn't want to, he eased away from her. "Better answer."

"Yeah." Gulping for air, she turned to the wheelbarrow and pulled her phone out of her jacket pocket. "It's Kendra." She took a deep breath and tapped the screen. "Hi!" She cleared her throat. "How're you guys?"

Aleck made do with half of the conversation, but it was enough to tell him something was about to happen involving horses.

"You bet." She nodded and glanced at him. "I have another thought, though. Instead of me leading Diablo to Ryker and April's, what if Aleck rode him over there?"

He blinked. *What the hell*?

She gave him a quick smile. "He'll be fine. He's an athlete. I'll bet he'd love it."

<u>16</u>

"What in the name of all that's holy are you suggestin', lass?" Aleck stared at her as if she'd lost her mind.

"You don't have to do it." Tansy reached under her shirt and fastened her bra. "But it's a way for us to end up in my apartment for a couple of hours."

Oh. "Then I'd best hear what you've cooked up."

"Quinn's road is washed out and his hardly ever floods, which means Wild Creek's will be way worse. It'll be a while before vehicles can drive on either one. All four grandparents are saddling up to ride over here to check on the new family."

"What about the wee bairn, Noel? Are they bringin' her?"

She shook her head. "Don't have to. Cody and Faith made it to Quinn's last night. They got stuck on his road and had to hike the rest of the way, but they're with Noel."

"Well, that's good."

"It is, but Rory and Damaris are still in town and they really want to come home this morning. Damaris needs her computer and Rory wants to be here to help with barn chores. The work is more complicated when it rains this much."

"So Kendra asked you to take them a couple of horses to ride home on?"

"Exactly. She already checked with them and they'd be very happy if I'd agree to do that. I can borrow their truck to drive to the GG and when the road dries out, they'll bring mine to town and we'll switch out again."

He gazed at her, clearly turning it all over in his mind. "And how long do you think it'll take for the road to dry out?"

"I don't know. I can't hear the rain anymore, so maybe the storm's over. If the sun comes out, the road might be dry enough later today. Kendra could answer that better than I can."

"A ride to town sounds like more than a wee outing."

"Actually, it's not. There's a shortcut to town through the woods. Kendra and I have gone that way lots of times when we felt like getting a treat at Pie in the Sky."

Aleck's brow furrowed. "How long would it take?"

"We can make it in under twenty minutes, even going slow. I know you're uneasy about the riding, but think of the advantages. At the end of the ride we'll pick up Rory's truck and be in my apartment about ten minutes later."

Heat flared in his gaze. "That part sounds—"

"Pure barry?"

"Aye, it does. But if my baws have been jostled every which way on the back of that horse because I don't know the proper way to ride, I might not be in any shape to enjoy it."

"I promise I won't let that happen. I have a stake in the outcome so I'll keep checking on you to make sure you're feeling comfy."

He still looked unconvinced.

"This won't be as hard as you think. Way easier than a caber toss. Like I told Kendra, you're an athlete. Twenty minutes is doable, even for a beginner." But he didn't like being a beginner. She could see it in his eyes.

He was silent for a few seconds. Then he gave a short nod. "All right, then, lass. I'll put myself in your hands."

"Mm. I like the sound of that."

His breath caught. "I hope you know you're drivin' me crazy."

"No more than you're doing to me."

He groaned softly and glanced away, shoving his hands in his pockets. "Lord give me strength." He took several deep breaths before turning back to her. "What's next?"

"We lead Diablo and Strawberry out to the wash rack pad and saddle them there."

"Wash rack pad?"

"It's a cement area on one side of the barn where they bathe the horses. We don't want them standing in the mud while we saddle them."

"I want to help with the saddlin'."

"Good." Evidently once he committed to something new, he wanted all the info he could get. Saddling his own horse was a great way to demystify the process. "I'll get us a couple of lead ropes."

"I'd like to lead my horse out there, too."

She paused, surprised and delighted with the request. "Absolutely." She was also tickled that he'd referred to Diablo as *my horse.* She glanced into Strawberry's stall to make sure he'd finished his breakfast. "I'll take Strawberry first so you can see how I do it. Be right back with the ropes."

She returned with them, handed him one and opened Strawberry's stall door. She gave a running commentary as she attached the lead rope and brought the gelding out into the barn aisle. To say Aleck watched her every move was an understatement. His intense scrutiny created an electric vibration, leaving her alert...and aroused.

He walked beside her as she led the roan gelding out of the barn and tethered him to the wash rack's hitching post. When it was his turn to take Diablo out, he copied everything she'd done, including making occasional comments to the horse. She hadn't been conscious of doing it with Strawberry, but Aleck had noticed every detail.

He tethered the horse to the hitching post, gave him a scratch under his mane and turned back to her. "What now?"

"Grooming." Setting down the tote she'd grabbed on the way out of the barn, she picked up one brush and handed him the other. "Begin on the left side and work your way around." She started brushing and his gaze intensified as it had when she'd demonstrated leading. "The pressure should be gentle but firm."

He made a humming noise low in his throat.

She paused to glance at him. "What?"

"What you just said reminded me of somethin' I'm tryin' to put out of my mind for now."

A flush crept over her skin. "You'd better, or we won't be ready to leave when Kendra and crew arrive."

"I know that, lass. Usin' all my powers of concentration. Carry on."

"Not much more to it. Don't press too hard on the bony parts." She groaned. "Sorry."

"Dinna fash yourself. My mind was already goin' there." He started brushing Diablo.

After a few minutes, she glanced across Strawberry's broad back to check on Aleck's progress. Sure, that's why she was looking over there. It had nothing to do with the play of muscles under his shirt as he applied *gentle but firm* strokes to Diablo's coat.

Her core muscles clenched. Time to take her own advice and calm the heck down. Was there anything about him that didn't give her heart palpitations? Nope, he was a fine specimen of manhood from head to toe.

Oh, wait. His clunky rain boots didn't turn her on, and they needed to go. "We'll grab your cowboy boots before we leave. You need a better heel to help keep your feet in the stirrups. You'll want your hat, too."

He squinted up at a slight break in the clouds. "I'll wear my hat, but I'd hate to get mud on those fine boots Rory bought me."

"You won't get much. We can ride up to the end of the flagstone walk. But they're boots. If Rory were here, he'd tell you...what was that you said? Don't fash yourself?"

"That's what I said. Interestin' to hear it with a Boston accent."

"You get the idea, though, right?"

"I do." He blew out a breath. "I'll wear the boots."

She moved to Strawberry's right side, which robbed her of a visual on Aleck. Now he had one of her backside. Was he looking?

Another of his deep hums told her he was. She moved faster, galvanized by the promise of what the day could bring. "I'll get the tack."

"I'll come with you. I'm finished, too."

"Then we can put the tote back." She waited for him to drop his brush in it. "You must have turned on the afterburners to be done that quick." She picked up the tote and headed around to the front of the barn.

"I just kept pace with you." He fell into step beside her.

"I predict you're going to be very good at this. I can see why you've had success as a lawyer."

"How do you know I have?"

"Well, you said you love it, and that usually means a person's successful. You also have an extraordinary eye for detail. Clearly you've found your path."

"And you've found yours, it seems."

"I have."

"I'm happy for you, lass. Glad you found a place where you can thrive. And you are thrivin'. That might be why I—" He paused.

"What?"

"I've been tryin' to analyze why I'm so...affected by you."

"Affected? That sounds like a disease."

He laughed. "Sometimes it feels like I'm comin' down with somethin'. It's just that I want you so much...more than I've ever..." He took a deep breath and met her gaze.

Holy hot Scot. The fire in those green eyes would melt her panties in no time.

His chest heaved again. "We need to get those horses saddled."

"Yes. Yes, we do." Assuming she had enough working brain cells to accomplish it.

17

Aleck used his honed ability to concentrate as he'd never used it before. By the time Tansy had instructed him in saddling and bridling a horse, he could have taught a class in it.

The unfamiliar task had been a welcome challenge that had steadied his runaway heartbeat and calmed his restless tadger. He hadn't been so out of control since…ever.

Rory was the impulsive one, the guy who'd often ended up in a guddle because he hadn't paused to consider the ramifications of his behavior. True, his latest escapade had resulted in finding the love of his life. Then again, he'd been in a position to change his circumstances.

Aleck had no wish to change anything. He had friends, family and his dream job. He loved Scotland and planned to live there forever. So why had he eagerly climbed aboard a horse named Diablo for the sole purpose of ending up in an American girl's apartment? Making love to her was not in line with the path he'd laid out for himself.

But he was going to do it, anyway. Because...Tansy. He had no other excuse. One glance into her brown eyes and he was lost.

Mounting the reddish horse named Strawberry with practiced ease, she led the way over to the house so he could get his hat and boots. Their horses' hooves squished in the mud as he followed her to the rail fence that stretched on either side of the flagstone path.

Swiveling in her saddle, she glanced back at him. "Come up on my left side so you'll be closer to the walkway."

He nudged Diablo in the ribs and neck-reined him the way Tansy had taught him before they'd left the barn area. It wasn't the best parking job in the world, but it would do. When he pulled gently on the reins, Diablo stopped. "Brakes work. Steering wheel needs some adjustin'."

"You'll get the hang of it." She climbed down and looped Strawberry's reins around the railing. "Get off on the left."

"I remember." He used the horn to steady himself during the dismount. It would likely save him from disaster during this adventure. He might be a numptie when it came to riding a horse, but he had a grip like iron.

After looping Diablo's reins around the railing like Tansy had, he joined her on the walkway.

"You're doing great, by the way."

"Thanks."

"How does the saddle feel?"

"Better than I expected. Not as comfy as an easy chair, though."

"Give yourself time and you might prefer it to an easy chair."

He smiled. "Doubtful." He climbed the steps. "I need to take off these boots before I go in."

"Right. I'll wait for you on the porch." She sat in the second rocker over from the door.

As he claimed the one beside her and tugged off his first boot, his stomach growled.

She glanced at him. "Hungry?"

"Pay me no mind, lass." He set the boot beside his chair.

"I'm not surprised if you are. So am I. We should each grab something."

"Sounds like fun." He chuckled and took off his other boot.

"I'm talking about food."

He glanced at her. "I'm not."

Her breathing changed. "You really have to stop looking at me like that."

"Can't help it."

She held his gaze for a moment longer. "Go get your stuff." Her voice was low and throaty. "Before I forget myself and kiss you."

"I'd like that."

"Go."

"Aye, right." He pushed himself out of his chair.

"Meanwhile I'll see what I can find in the kitchen that will be quick and easy." She pulled off her boots and stood. "We don't want to arrive at my apartment faint with hunger."

"I promise food will be the furthest thing from my mind, whether I eat somethin' now or not."

"Even so, we should…" She paused. "I hear horses." Turning, she looked across the yard toward the empty pasture. "Must be the grandparent brigade." She rose on tiptoe and pointed. "There they are. See 'em?"

"Aye. Comin' along the fence."

She grinned. "They're making tracks, too. No washed-out road is keeping them from their grandbaby. That's Kendra out in front. Bet it was her idea to ride over here." She waved and Kendra waved back.

"Does she keep a horse over at Quinn's place, then?"

"No, she's on Fudge, Wes's horse."

"And Wes is…?"

"Quinn's youngest son. I keep forgetting you haven't met his kids. You will. Wes is a horse vet and he stables his horse at his dad's."

"Quinn's horse is an interestin' color."

"Banjo is a buckskin."

"Fudge and Banjo. I almost want a horse so I can name him."

"Aha! You're getting into this. I thought you would."

"I said *almost.* The names are fascinatin'. What are Jo and Brendan's horses called?"

"Don't know. First time I've seen them. They got them last month."

"Jo's looks like a happier, taller version of Eeyore."

"Yeah, he's handsome, all right. She's been sharing Eeyore with Mandy, so it's not surprising she wanted a gray. Looks awesome with Brendan's roan. His horse and Strawberry would almost make a matched pair."

"I used to think of all horses as being brown, like Diablo."

"It's the most common color, but as you can tell from this bunch, it's not the only one. It's cool to see all the variations." She sighed. "I love these animals."

"Want one?"

"Definitely, but not until I can afford my own place where I can keep a horse. I'm saving up."

"Sounds excitin'." All these specific plans—Rory wanting a house and kids, Tansy saving for a horse and her own place--were vaguely annoying. What were his? Surely he had some.

"Hey, you two!" Aunt Kendra parked Fudge next to Strawberry and Quinn pulled Banjo in alongside her.

"You made good time." Tansy glanced over at Brendan and Jo as they rode up to the other side of the fence and dismounted. "Beautiful horses!"

"Aren't they?" Jo patted the neck of her dapple gray. "This is Mercury and that's Mars." She pointed to Brendan's horse. "I wanted to name mine Venus, because that would be cute to have Mars and Venus, but I finally decided he wouldn't like having a girl's name."

"Thank the Lord." Aleck gave Jo a thumbs-up. "Sanity prevails."

"Bonnie and Clyde didn't sit well with Aleck." Tansy sent a wink in his direction.

"That trips up a lot of folks, Aleck." Aunt Kendra smiled at him as she started up the walkway. "Looks like you decided to ride Diablo over to Ryker and April's."

"Aye. That I did."

Approval shone in her eyes. "Good for you."

"And he groomed and tacked up that horse, too," Tansy said.

Quinn nodded. "Good man."

"Appreciate the compliment, but I get the impression that's standard procedure around here."

"It is." Jo followed Aunt Kendra and Quinn up the walkway with Brendan right behind her. "That's how Kendra got me over my fear. You must not have any since you've jumped right in like that."

"I'm not afraid of the horse. Just worried that I'll end up on my bum my first time out."

Quinn smiled. "That's the mark of a good fall, son. If you're coming off, it's best to land on the seat of your pants. There's no disgrace in falling. We've all done it."

"*All* of you?" Everyone nodded. "Am I supposed to find that comfortin'?"

"You're not going to fall." Tansy reached over and squeezed his arm. "And even if you do, we'll be going so slow it won't matter."

"Sorry, but I don't find that comfortin' either, lass."

"Enough." Aunt Kendra came up on the porch. "We're freaking him out when there's no reason. It's an easy ride and Tansy knows the route. Did you two get some breakfast, by the way?"

"We didn't," Tansy said. "And we probably should eat something before we go."

Aunt Kendra's eyebrows lifted. "You're kidding, right? There's no *probably* in that sentence. Come inside and we'll get you fed. Do you know if Zane and Mandy have had anything to eat this morning?"

"We have not." Rubbing his eyes, Zane walked out on the porch in his bare feet. "Are you guys having a party or what?"

"Oh, honey." Aunt Kendra gave him a kiss on his beard-roughened cheek. "Did we wake you?"

"Yes, but I don't care. I'm so freaking glad to see you. With the road out, I was afraid—"

Jo gasped. "Is something wrong?"

"Nothing's wrong. Mandy and I just need..." He cleared his throat and his gaze swept the group. "We need our family."

Such a declaration of vulnerability from a rock of a man like Zane took Aleck's breath away. The outpouring of love and hugs that followed created a sizable lump in his throat.

When Rory and Damaris started their family, they'd be surrounded by the same warm circle of caring folks. It was good to know. But his chest hurt, all the same.

_18_

Breakfast was a quick affair, for which Tansy was grateful. Aleck seemed to be, too. He clearly wanted to get on with it. The sooner they made this ride he was nervous about and progressed to the good part, the better.

After breakfast, Kendra found a hat for her to wear. Rhys woke up right before they were ready to leave, so they had a chance to see the little guy. Then they left without fanfare since everyone was fully occupied with the baby.

She waited for Aleck to climb aboard Diablo before she mounted up. Once he was in the saddle, she checked his stirrups and asked him to stand in them so she could make sure the clearance was optimal.

That required focusing on the very region of his body that had fueled some sizzling fantasies recently. The denim of his jeans contained, but didn't fully conceal, what lay in store for her.

Stop staring, Tansy. She gulped and looked away, but it was too late. Heat spiraled through her belly and moistened her lady parts. "You're fine," she murmured. *Mighty fine.* "Go ahead and sit down."

"It's nice to be appreciated, lass."

She lifted her gaze to smiling green eyes shaded by a black Stetson. Killer combination. "I need to..." What? Oh, yeah. "I have to lead, but please call out if you have a problem."

"I already have one."

"What?"

"We're not at your apartment yet."

She took a shaky breath. "We will be before you know it."

He just grinned. "If you believe that, your head's full o' mince. This will be the longest twenty minutes in history."

"Yeah, it will." She ducked under Diablo's neck, unwound Strawberry's reins from the rail and swung into the saddle. "Follow me." She turned the gelding and headed toward the break between the barn and the pasture fence. Swiveling in the saddle, she glanced back at Aleck. "Heels down, cowboy."

He shoved them down. "Cowboy?"

"No? You're wearing the hat and the boots, sitting in a Western saddle on a horse born and raised in Montana. Despite misgivings, you're riding out to give aid to a stranded member of your family."

"My primary motivation is gettin' to spend time with a lovely lass."

"That's the clincher. You have the clothes, the horse, the challenging task and the girl at the end of the trail. I hereby pronounce you a cowboy." She faced forward as his soft laughter drifted up to her, warming her all over.

Strawberry picked his way along the muddy trail, but as it sloped upward toward the pines, the footing improved. She turned to see how Aleck was getting along.

Better than she could have hoped. Instead of sitting frozen in the saddle, he was clearly entranced by the view. As the horses made their way upward, the sun obligingly broke through the clouds.

Distinct beams fanned out with light-show drama, illuminating the flanks of the snow-tipped mountains and strewing glitter on the grass and wildflowers in the meadow. Glorious. Exactly what she would have wished for Aleck's first ride.

"Can we stop?"

"Sure." She pulled back on the reins.

"I want to take a picture. This is spectacular."

"Can't argue with that." She turned Strawberry to face him. "Loop your reins over the horn."

"Done." He took his phone from his pocket. "Maybe I'll take a video. That would capture it better." He swiveled in the saddle and slowly rotated back toward her, holding the camera steady. Focusing on her, he waved. She smiled and waved back.

Then he panned in reverse, turning so far the other way that he lost his left stirrup.

"Aleck, you'd better—"

Too late. He's already begun to slide. In trying to right himself, he lost the other stirrup. He grabbed for the horn. Missed.

She vaulted from her saddle and got there shortly after he landed. By some miracle his tush hit a patch of wet grass instead of mud.

"Are you okay?"

He looked up and grinned. "My pride hurts like hell."

"Hey, it's easy to get distracted by this view." She held out her hand and pulled him to his feet.

"That I did, lass." He located his Stetson a few feet away and walked over to retrieve it. "Hat looks okay." He tapped it against his thigh to dislodge a few blades of grass before putting it on. "How's the seat of my pants?"

"Just some grass. No mud. You were lucky." She didn't allow her attention to linger there as he brushed the wet grass away.

"Did I get it all?"

"Yep."

He held up his phone. "At least I hung onto this. Before we mount up again, let's look." He clicked on the video and held the phone so they could both see. "Amazin' sunbeams. That's what made me want to stop."

"You really captured them." Standing this close to him messed with her breathing, but she wanted to share in his excitement. "You got the sparkles on the wildflowers, too."

"Aye. And there's you. Now I'm goin' back the other way. Disaster's about to strike...and I'm on the ground." He started laughing. "I even videoed the slide down. Finally thought to turn it off." He drew in a breath. "Great souvenir."

She glanced at him. "So now that you've moved around a little, still no aches and pains?"

He met her gaze. "Oh, I ache, lass, but not from comin' off the horse. We'd best be gettin' back on, too, before I kiss that rosy pink mouth and lose my mind."

Heat surged through her. "Right." She put a little distance between them. "Are you nervous about getting back on?"

He pocketed his phone. "Should I be?"

"No, but sometimes people are after they've taken a fall."

"For me, it's a relief. I'm almost lookin' forward to the rest of the ride now that I'm past that."

She nodded. "Okay, then. Let's ride." Walking back to Strawberry, she mounted up. Sure enough, Aleck did look more relaxed as he climbed aboard Diablo and unlooped the reins from the saddle horn. "We'll be going through the trees soon. Not as many photo ops."

"Just as well."

She turned Strawberry around. "We're off, then. Next stop, April and Ryker's house."

* * *

Aleck wouldn't say he loved riding, exactly, but seeing the natural world from the back of a horse had advantages. He'd taken long rambles through the moors, but on horseback he could cover more territory and have a better view.

Truth be told, he hadn't taken one of those rambles in months. Could even be a couple of years. The air smelled good out here. A picnic would be nice. A picnic involving Tansy would be *very* nice. Likely wouldn't be time.

She pointed out landmarks along the way and kept asking him how he was doing. Fine, just fine. He shifted in the saddle every now and then to make sure. But relaxed as he was, he shouldn't have an issue.

Sharing the journey with an animal gave the trek an added richness, as if he had a closer connection to the earth and the creatures on it. Whenever he spoke, Diablo swiveled his ears back to catch the conversation. Aleck dreamed up things to talk about just to watch those ears rotate. Damned endearing.

The trail emerged from the forest into civilization. Houses were sparse at first, but eventually the trail skirted the backside of a neighborhood. Still rural, though. Folks had goats and chickens in their yards and pickup trucks were the most popular choice of vehicle.

"I just texted April and Ryker," Tansy said. "We're almost there."

"Which is theirs?"

"Three houses up. Look for the chicken coop in the backyard."

"Ah. I see it." The brightly painted coop looked more like a child's elaborate dollhouse than a home for laying hens. Aunt Kendra's was easily as grand as this one. "Does everyone in the family have fancy chicken coops?"

"Not everyone, but it's catching on. Trevor built one for Olivia, and now Jo wants one."

"Not Zane and Mandy?"

She laughed. "Zane seems to think having all those birds of prey nearby would give the chickens so much anxiety they wouldn't lay a single egg. Kendra keeps them supplied, though."

"My grandparents have chickens, but the coops don't look like that."

"Not many do." She stood in her stirrups and waved. "The cavalry has arrived!"

"Hang on!" Ryker called out. "Forgot we needed to get these chickens inside the pen before we can open the gate."

"No worries. We'll wait." She rode up to the edge of the solid wooden fence that bordered the yard.

Aleck came up beside her. "Saints alive." Rory, Damaris, Ryker, April and a guy he didn't recognize chased after more squawking chickens than he could count. He smiled. "This is worth the price of admission."

"I know, right?" She raised her voice. "We could ride to the end of the block and come up the street!"

"No, no." Ryker was breathing hard as he charged after a handsome rooster with glossy black feathers. "Prince Charming's the last one. Head him off, Rory."

"He's comin' toward Damaris, not me."

"Much more of this and I'm getting my rope. I know you cherish this son-of-a-bucket, April, but I'm ready to—"

"He's a sweetheart, Ryker!" April dodged left and right, trying to catch the rooster.

"He's not a sweetheart. He's—"

"I'll get him, Cowboy." The man Aleck couldn't identify made a dive for the rooster and came up with his arms full of a flapping, squawking, clearly ticked off rooster.

"Thanks, Raven." Ryker blew out a breath. "Dump him in the pen."

"Don't you dare dump him," April said. "Set him down gently. He makes my hens very happy."

"All clear?" Rory backed toward the gate. "Can I let 'em in?"

"All clear." Ryker took off his hat and wiped his face with a red bandana. "Prince Charming, my ass."

Rory unlatched the gate and swung it open. "Thanks for doin' this, guys. Big brother, you look mighty fine on that horse."

"Ask Tansy how fine I looked sittin' in the dirt."

"Diablo threw you? I can't believe he'd—"

"My fault entirely." Aleck patted Diablo's neck. "If I'd been payin' better attention, it wouldn't have happened."

"You're all right, though? Nothin' bruised or broken?"

"Only my manly image." He rode into the yard. "He's a good horse." When Rory took hold of the bridle, he climbed down. No ill effects, thank the Lord.

"Yeah, he's a very good horse." Rory stroked his muzzle and then led him over to a grassy section of the yard where Strawberry was already grazing. "Other than takin' a tumble, how was it?"

"I...um, I liked it."

"See?" Rory's smile was a mile wide. "I knew you would." He glanced over at Tansy, who was talking to Damaris and April. "He said he *liked* it."

"I thought so." She turned to Aleck. "All you need is more practice and you'll have it down."

"But—"

"That's for sure," Rory said. "You're good at whatever you put your mind to."

"I can believe that." Ryker came over with the guy who'd caught the rooster. "Hey, Aleck, you haven't met my buddy Raven."

"Glad to finally meet you, Aleck." He offered his hand. "Heard a lot about you from Rory."

Aleck grasped his hand. "That lands me in a guddle, because I—"

"You have no idea who I am." Amusement flashed in his gray eyes. "Aaron Donahue."

"Why does Ryker call you Raven?"

"Squadron nickname. We served together in the Air Force and then Cowboy hired me to work with him at Badger Air."

"Who's Cowboy?"

"Me," Ryker said. "That was my nickname."

"And I can't get used to calling him anything else," Aaron said. "But seems like every guy around here's a cowboy, so it gets confusing."

"I'm not."

He smiled. "That's what I said when I moved here." He nudged back his Stetson. "Take my word for it, hang with this bunch and you'll start thinking of yourself that way before long."

"Likely I won't transform by Friday. That's when I'm leavin'."

"Seems a shame after coming all this way," Ryker said. "It barely leaves time for our rematch."

"No rematch!" Tansy called out.

Ryker grinned. "Just kidding, Tansy! I do wish you could stay longer, though."

"Me, too."

"But I know you can't." Rory heaved a sigh. "I'll just start plannin' for the next visit."

"So will I." Aleck didn't look at Tansy, but she was still in his peripheral vision, talking with April and Damaris. She'd taken off her hat and sunlight gleamed in the multicolored strands of her hair.

On Friday, he'd put an ocean between them. The logical concept fit into his brain. But he was no longer certain there was room for it in his heart.

<u>19</u>

When April had to take a call from a massage client who wanted to book an appointment, Tansy and Damaris had a moment alone.

Damaris moved closer and lowered her voice. "As you saw, Rory's thrilled that you got his brother on a horse. When Kendra dreamed up this idea, he almost texted you to suggest having Aleck ride Diablo over here. Clearly you were way ahead of him."

"I have ulterior motives for getting him to town."

"We figured that out." Damaris pushed her glasses more firmly against the bridge of her nose. "Rory's alerted Michael and Bryce to pay no attention if you and Aleck slip in the back door and up the stairs."

"Sheesh. So much for clandestine."

"Yes, but you know those guys. If Rory didn't say something, they'd be all *hey, Tansy and Aleck! What's up? Want a burger and fries?*"

Tansy smiled. "They would, and thank Rory for giving them the word. I hadn't factored that in. They'll both be at the GG stockpiling supplies for Thursday. But that brings up another point. Aleck came to see his brother but now he'll be spending the afternoon with me."

"Because he wants to, right?"

"Yes, but—"

"Rory's fine with that. More than fine. He heard something different in Aleck's voice when he talked about you yesterday."

"He did?" That news jacked up her pulse. "Like what?"

Damaris shook her head. "I don't want to put too fine a point on it or plant ideas in your head. Just enjoy these few hours together and see where it leads."

"I already have ideas in my head. Aleck's a very special guy and I...yeah, there's something different about the way I think of him, too. But when I'm honest with myself, I can't see how—"

"I know. Neither can I. And yet, look at what happened with me and Rory."

"Aleck's not Rory and I'm not you."

"Good thing! How confusing would that be? Just go have fun, okay?"

"Okay."

Not long afterward, Tansy drove away from April and Ryker's house with Aleck in the passenger seat. "This truck feels ginormous." She navigated cautiously through traffic.

"You're doin' a better job than I would. Rented a car in Paris once. Had to battle heavy traffic plus bein' on a different side from what I was used to. It's a wonder I survived."

"I'm really glad you did."

"I'm *very* glad." He glanced at her. "Especially today." Tenderness softened his words.

Was he falling for her? Was that even possible in such a short time? Was she falling for him? She took a shaky breath. "This isn't a romantic subject, but there's a drugstore, Pills and Pop, on Main Street."

"Aye. Rory pointed it out on the drive in."

"Do we need to stop?"

"Do you want me to buy a razor, lass?"

"Not on your life. Your beard is just getting nice. I'm talking about birth control. There's a coin-operated dispenser in the men's room at the GG, but—"

"We don't have to stop and I don't need the dispenser. I'm well supplied."

"You are?"

"The McGavin clan believes in share and share alike."

"Oh." Made her giggle.

"Rory told me to go have fun."

"Damaris told me the same thing, although she didn't supply me with birth control. They've also informed Bryce and Michael that we'll be sneaking in the back way so they should ignore us."

"Guess we have everyone's blessin', then. That's somethin'. But I'm not used to conductin' my private life in the public eye. Makes me a wee bit self-conscious."

"We don't have to go to my apartment. I could show you around town instead."

"It doesn't make me *that* self-conscious."

"Just checking. I'll park in the back." She maneuvered around the building. "Damn, this thing is huge. I usually back in because it's so much easier to drive out again, but I'm afraid I'll hit the dumpster." She put on the brakes. "Would you get out and direct me?"

"Aye, glad to." He unfastened his seat belt, hopped out and closed the door.

After lowering both windows, she pulled the massive vehicle around and located Aleck in her side mirror.

He beckoned to her. "Come on back."

She put the truck in reverse and eased slowly toward him.

"Go left."

She turned the wheel.

"Good. Straighten it out. Keep comin', keep comin'...stop."

After turning off the engine, she left her borrowed hat on the dash. It needed to go back to Wild Creek and this way she wouldn't forget in the excitement of having Aleck in her apartment.

She tucked the keys under the seat, climbed out and glanced at her proximity to the dumpster. A good two feet of clearance. Perfect. She turned. "Thanks for the help."

He nudged back his hat and smiled at her. "You're welcome. Beautiful job, lass."

Beautiful man. Speechless, she drank in the magnificence of Aleck McGavin—caring, loyal, giving...and sexy as hell. The truth slammed into her, leaving her shaken. She wasn't falling for him. She'd fallen.

* * *

Aleck's breath caught. In the brief span of time he'd known Tansy, he'd savored the changing emotions on her lovely face—determination, amusement, concern, patience, frustration, joy, passion. But she'd never looked at him like this.

His chest swelled and his throat grew tight. Her gaze mirrored the certainty churning through him. Her reality became his. *Now we know, Tansy-girl. Now we know where we are.*

The GG's back door opened and Michael came out with a bulging garbage bag in each hand. He stopped. "Hey, guys."

"Hi, Michael." Tansy's voice squeaked. "Aleck and I were just—"

"Let me give you a hand with those." Aleck stepped forward, took one of the bags and lifted the lid of the dumpster so he could toss it in. Then he held it open so Michael could throw in the other one.

"Thanks, Aleck. The glamorous life of a business owner never ends." He paused. "Are you two coming in, then?"

"Yes." Tansy's cheeks were pink. "Yes, we are."

"Then allow me." Michael opened the door for them. "Probably shouldn't say this, but you're stirring up some great memories for me."

Aleck glanced at him as he walked into the building. "How's that?"

"He used to live upstairs," Tansy said.

"Sure did." Michael came in and closed the door. "That's where Roxanne and I...well, like I said, great memories."

Aleck stared at him in total confusion. "I have no idea what to do with that information."

"Just letting you know the place has good vibes." Michael grinned. "Have fun." He tipped his hat and walked into the GG dining room where the lunch crowd was already gathering.

Tansy turned to him. The depth of emotion he'd seen in her eyes a few moments ago had been replaced by a sparkle of laughter. She gestured toward a wooden staircase where a velvet rope blocked access. "Ready to go have fun?"

He shrugged, feigning nonchalance. "Seems like that's what everyone expects of us."

"No kidding." She stepped over to the rope and unhooked it. "Pressure's on. We'd better have fun or else." She headed up the stairs.

"I'm not too worried about it." Predictably, his jeans began to pinch as he followed her. "I've been having fun ever since I met you."

"Same here. But this is a different sort of fun."

"I'd call it the best sort."

"It can be. With the right person."

"Like I said, nothing to worry about."

20

Aleck followed Tansy into the apartment at the top of the stairs, turned and closed the door. The soft click jumpstarted his pulse.

Drawing in a breath, he took off his hat and hung it on the doorknob. Then he looked around.

Tansy kept her small living area shipshape, the way Aleck kept his. But there the similarity ended. Each wall was a different color. Brightly patterned curtains hung at the window and she'd used the same material for a cloth to cover her small dinette table and the cushions on each of the two chairs.

A tiny kitchen created an L shape at the far end of the apartment. The bed took up most of the remaining space and commanded nearly all his attention. The coverlet on her bed was a kaleidoscope of every shade in the rainbow.

He looked closer. The room was more than shipshape. Nothing was out of place. Even the coverlet on the bed was perfectly smooth. Not a single dent or wrinkle in the fabric.

She stood motionless in the middle of the room, calmly watching him.

"The place looks nice."

"Thank you."

"Almost as if you were expectin' someone."

"I was."

"Who would that be?"

"You."

He blinked. "But we just came up with our plan today."

"I've been imagining you in my apartment ever since you walked in the door of the GG."

"Hey, now. That's...I like hearin' that, lass."

"Remember when you asked if I lived upstairs?"

"Aye."

"I wanted to say *you're welcome anytime.* I didn't know if it would ever happen, but I've been keeping the place picked up since then, just in case."

"And here I am."

"And it's like I imagined, only better."

He walked toward her, taking his time. "We've been on the same page all along."

"You imagined yourself in my apartment?"

"Couldn't since I'd never seen it. I just knew that somehow I had to find a way that we could be alone." He cupped her face in both hands. "From the moment I looked into your eyes, I knew..." He paused to draw a breath. "Knew I had to make love to you."

Reaching up, she cradled his head and held his gaze. "Then please do."

The glow in her eyes was back, shining so brightly that his heart ached. He lowered his mouth to hers.

Ahhh. Sinking under waves of delight, he surrendered at last to the needs that buffeted him whenever she was near. Her kiss urged him on. Her moans fired his blood.

He undressed her with hands made clumsy with haste. Breathing hard, she fumbled with his shirt buttons, swore softly when she couldn't undo his jeans fast enough. Frustration gave way to laughter as they were nearly defeated by their boots.

After an eternity of struggling to free themselves from the trap of jeans and boots, they tumbled onto her multi-colored coverlet gasping for breath. He moved over her and braced himself on his outstretched arms.

"I want to look at you, lass." He gulped for air. "So bonnie lyin' on this riot of color. A feast for the eyes, you are."

"Feast away."

"I must warn you, I have a powerful appetite."

She ran her hands over his pecs, lightly stroking his sensitized skin and teasing his chest hair. "I like that in a man."

"Somehow I knew that about you." Leaning down, he pressed his mouth against the hollow of her throat. The quick tattoo of her pulse vibrated against his lips for a moment.

Slowly, deliberately, he began his journey, a quest to learn all he could about the woman who had bedeviled him. Along the way he intended to ratchet up that drumbeat. He wouldn't stop until she was writhing in the grip of the same insatiable desire burning in his loins.

That assumed he could explore her quivering body without giving in to his own needs. Maybe not. As he traveled, her breathing kept pace with his progress. He made sweet love to her breasts before kissing a trail down each arm, paying close attention to the tender spot inside her elbow.

Ah, but his tadger and his baws paid the toll on this road of discovery. He silently promised them their eventual reward. The wait would be worth it.

Bypassing his main goal, he concentrated on her feet with her patriotic toenails. She was ticklish. Made him smile. Nor did he take advantage. He was ticklish, too.

The backs of her knees were sensitive to the slow swipe of his tongue. Her thighs even more so. As he made his way to her inner thighs and gradually moved higher, she gasped out his name.

He nibbled closer, breathing in the intoxicating scent of arousal. "What, lass?"

"Please."

"Aye." Sliding both hands under her firm backside, he lifted her for the most intimate of all kisses.

Ah, now she was in the grip of it, moaning and twisting on the coverlet as he brought her to the brink and hurled her over it. She muffled her long, lusty cry of release.

Lowering her back to the coverlet, he kissed his way up her flushed body, propped himself on his forearms, and gazed into her heavy-lidded eyes. "Having fun?"

She sucked in a breath. "Big fun."

"My turn." Sliding off the bed, he located his jeans and fished a condom out of the pocket.

"I'll...do my...best."

He lifted his eyebrows. "Concerning what?"

"To be fun. I'm...limp as a...banana peel."

He finished rolling on the condom and returned to the bed. "Dinna fash yourself, lass. My tadger and I will bring you back to life."

She smiled. "I could listen to you all day."

"And all night?" He moved between her thighs.

"That, too."

He ached something fierce, but he held back so he could check her beautiful face for whisker burn. "I see a wee bit of evidence of my beard."

"I don't care."

Bracing himself above her, he studied the smooth slope of her breasts. "Some there, too. I'll be more careful."

"Don't you dare be careful. The brush of your beard was erotic especially...at the end."

"Didn't think of that. Was just—"

"Driving me wild. If my thighs chafe a little during my shift tonight, I'll remember why."

Desire fisted in his gut. "Somethin' more I'd have you remember." He thrust deep.

She gasped. "I do...believe I will."

"So will I." Closing his eyes, he reveled in the sensation of her warm channel sheathing his tadger.

"Having fun?"

"Aye." He opened his eyes so he could watch the change in hers. "Can't remember ever havin' this much of it at one time."

"Me, either." She wrapped her arms around him. "Maybe it's the good vibes here."

"Could be."

"You agree?"

"Why not?" He took a chance and moved a wee bit. Didn't lose control. Moved a wee bit more.

"The lawyers I've known wouldn't."

"I'm a Scotsman." He eased back and pushed deep again.

Her breath hitched. "So?"

"Our national animal is the unicorn." He stroked more firmly. Got an answering quiver from her channel.

"It's...it's the lion."

"Do your research. It's both." He initiated a steady pace, even though his tadger wanted fire and fury. Tansy needed to catch up so she could ride the whirlwind with him.

"Didn't know that." Her breathing quickened.

"But I don't credit the vibes of this place."

"See? You don't really—"

"It's us." He took a chance and moved faster.

Her pupils widened. "You think?"

"I do, lass. I also think you're goin' to come again."

"Couldn't possibly."

"Is that a challenge?"

"Ah, right. You love a—"

"Challenge accepted." He shifted the angle and bore down.

"Oh, *my.*" Her fingertips pressed into his back.

Even better, her core muscles clenched. He had this. "Still limp as a banana?"

"Not...so much." She rose to meet his next thrust.

"Come when I come."

"I just might."

"Count on it." The pressure of an impending climax made him gasp. "We should...be quiet."

"Uh-huh." She began to pant. "If you can."

"I can." Her first spasm rippled over his rock-hard tadger. "Let go, Tansy-girl."

"Ah, Aleck...*Aleck.*" She pressed a fist to her mouth as she arched upward in a blaze of glory.

Her orgasm set off his. Teeth clenched against the bellow he had to swallow, his breath hissed out as his happy tadger celebrated with gusto. He quivered and shook. The room spun as if he'd been drinking all night. Somehow he managed not to collapse onto Tansy.

When the red haze cleared and he could see again, she was gazing up at him, her brow furrowed.

He peered closer. "Lass? You all right?"

"I'm fine. Great. Are *you* okay?"

"I'm spectacular."

"Whew, that's a relief. That was an epic reaction to a climax. Worried me some."

"Thought the top of my head was comin' off."

"That doesn't sound good."

He smiled. "Oh, no, that climax was braw."

"Is that like pure barry?"

"Aye. But I couldn't yell and carry on, so I stuffed it down. Took some effort. Probably looked like I was havin' a fit."

"Braw, huh?" She looked pleased about that.

"Best word for it. Any more intense and I might have blacked out."

"Wow. Is that how it usually is for you?"

He hesitated. Oh, what the hell. "No."

"Maybe it's the time change."

She was adorable. "It's not the time change. It's you."

"Me? I didn't do anything."

"Except be your wonderful self. But I stand corrected. It's not only you." He dipped his head and brushed a light kiss over her mouth. "It's us."

21

While Aleck was in the bathroom taking care of the condom, Tansy threw on a filmy cover-up she used to wear when she'd lived back East and had spent weekends at the beach. She hadn't worn it since moving to Eagles Nest, but it was perfect for walking around her apartment while entertaining a lover.

What a concept. Although she'd dated a few guys since relocating, none of them had excited her enough to justify inviting them up here. Aleck was the first. After the height of the bar he'd set, she couldn't imagine inviting anyone else.

She should feed the guy, though. He'd expended a lot of energy on her behalf. She was hungry, too. Rummaging through her small fridge yielded a tub of potato salad and a couple of baked chicken breasts, a quarter of a cherry pie from Pie in the Sky and a quart of vanilla ice cream.

He came out of the bathroom wearing nothing. It was a good look for him. If he wanted to stay like that, she wouldn't object in the slightest.

But one glance at her and he reached for his jeans and briefs.

"You don't have to put on clothes while we have something to eat."

"You did."

"This isn't clothes. You can see through it."

"Noticed that." A gleam lit his green eyes. "Enjoyin' the fact." He put on his knit briefs.

Although they hugged his package in a tempting way, she missed the full monty. "I enjoy seeing you without any clothes at all."

"Thank you for that, lass, but I'll put these on for sittin' at your wee table havin' some lunch. After that I'll be more than willin' to strip down again." He buttoned his jeans and zipped the fly.

"Okay." She smiled. "There's something to be said for that look, too. Same outfit you were wearing this morning when I walked out of the bathroom."

"Wearin' only a towel." He walked toward her. "Were you meanin' to drive me crazy?"

"No! I'd left my clean clothes in my room. How did I know you'd be leaning in your doorway waiting for me to come out?"

"After that kiss the night before, you didn't expect me to be there with my tongue hangin' out?"

"I didn't think that you—"

"You lit a fire in me." He pulled her close. "Leanin' in the doorway was all I could get away with. Wanted to come in and join you in the shower."

"Wish you could've." She wound her arms around his neck and snuggled against his bare chest. "I'd like showering with you."

"Checked out your wee shower just now. Sharin' it would take some doin'."

"I'm not sure we'd both fit, let alone have room to…have fun."

His eyes darkened. "Now I'm cravin' that experience with you."

"Not in the cards this trip."

He studied her silently for a moment, his expression unreadable. "Aye, can't be greedy."

"I'm afraid that's exactly what I am." She ran her finger around his sculpted lips.

"Want to forget about lunch?" He caught her hand and nibbled on her finger. "I could feast on you, again."

"Or I could feast on you."

He hummed low in his throat and pulled her in tight. "Sounds great. Let's—"

"But we should eat lunch. I'm not sending you back to Wild Creek hungry."

"Ask me if I care."

"I care." She wiggled out of his arms. "I have cold chicken and potato salad. I could warm up the chicken if you'd—"

"I'd rather not take the time."

"Good call." She opened the fridge so she could pull out the containers of food. "I also have cherry pie and ice cream if you want dessert."

"I definitely want dessert, but I have somethin' else in mind."

Desire curled and stretched, warming her core. He'd loved her so thoroughly already. What other treats did he have in store? Would he—

"Reconsiderin' the lunch plan?" He slid his arm around her waist and placed a kiss on her shoulder.

She snapped out of her daze and grabbed the container of potato salad. No telling how long she'd been standing in front of the fridge with the door wide open. "You can put that on the table, if you would, please."

He chuckled. "Sure thing."

"It's just that I'm not used to having a man in my apartment. I got distracted." She carried the container of chicken over to the counter and took two plates from the cupboard. "If you wouldn't mind, napkins are in that holder on the counter and silverware's in the drawer on my right."

"Happy to." He transferred both to the table and came back into the tiny kitchen area. "Do you consider Rory a man?"

She put a chicken breast on each plate. "Of course he's a man. What—"

"Just askin', because he told me that he and Damaris come up here and hang out with you sometimes. He said I'd like the place."

"You know what I mean." She handed him the plates.

"I do, lass. Just teasin' you. And thanks for the information, although I'm surprised. I'd think the men in this town would be beatin' a path to your door."

"I'm picky."

"Glad to hear it. And in case you couldn't tell, I feel honored to be here."

"I can tell." She gave him a smile.

"Quieter than I thought it would be up here. Cozy."

"There's usually a lull in the early afternoon. Want some McGavin Pale Ale to go with this?"

"Sure."

She took two bottles out of the fridge, twisted off the caps and brought them to the table. "Have a seat."

"First I'll get your chair." He came over, held it for her and scooted her in.

"Thanks."

"You're welcome." He took the other chair. "And just so you know, I didn't do that because Rory told me to. It's what I do for ladies back home."

"I'm sure they appreciate it." She wanted to ask about those ladies. Or did she? Maybe she wouldn't like what she heard.

He met her gaze across the table. "I'm picky, too." His expression wasn't difficult to read this time. He'd looked at her this way in the parking lot, right before Michael had come out.

Her heart beat faster. "Good to know."

"I want you to know. This...what's happened is...I don't usually..."

"Make love to someone the day after you've met?"

"Never."

"Neither have I. When I said I imagined you in my apartment the minute I saw you...I don't do that with men. But I did with you. I didn't even question it."

"No? I questioned the hell out of why I was respondin' this way to you."

"But it didn't stop you."

"Nothin' was goin' to stop me." He took a deep breath. "But it's only fair to tell you...I don't know where this is goin'." A small crease appeared between his brows.

"That's okay." She longed to smooth that frown away. "Don't fash yourself, lad."

His brow cleared and the light in his gaze intensified. He swallowed. "Tansy, I—"

"Aleck, don't." Her heart hammered so loud her ears buzzed.

"But—"

"This is brand new for both of us." *Breathe.* "You've questioned why it's happening. Makes sense that you would. I'm a complication in your world."

"And I'm not a complication in yours?"

"Not in the same way."

He hesitated, opened his mouth, closed it again. "I suppose not."

"We've moved really fast up to now."

"Aye."

"Now that we're at this point, maybe it's time to slow the hell down."

He blew out a breath. "There's wisdom in that, lass."

Grabbing her ale, she lifted it in his direction. "Let's drink to enjoying the moment."

He reached over and tapped his bottle against hers. "To enjoyin' *every* moment."

"Even better." She sipped her ale. "Damn, that's good stuff. Props to Rory."

Aleck took a healthy swallow and put down the bottle. "Rory's in his element here."

"He seems to be."

"No doubt about it." He tucked into his meal. "On the way in from the airport whenever he wasn't tryin' to convince me to get the hat, he was ravin' about the town and rhapsodizin' about Damaris."

"They're cute together." The food tasted great. Or maybe it was the company that added extra flavor. Aleck seemed to be enjoying his meal, too. Evidently she'd diffused the bomb he'd been about to drop.

He finished chewing and swallowed. "Cute is the word for it. He's crazy about her and she's just as nutty about him. With some couples, you can tell one person is more in love than the other. But they're equally besotted."

"She's even got him watching *Outlander*."

"He'd watch grass grow if she convinced him it was important to her."

She laughed. "Yeah, he would."

"He's changed a lot from the lad he was before he came over here." He put down his fork and took another sip of the ale.

"I believe it. I got a glimpse of that other Rory when he first arrived."

"There was a restlessness to him."

"Exactly."

"He managed to focus enough to get his degree and he was excited about workin' in a distillery, but his goals were vague." He forked up another bite of chicken. "Now he has a clear view of the future and what it'll take to get there."

"I'm going to guess you've always had that."

"Aye." The crease between his brows had returned. "Always." He didn't sound happy about it.

Damn. She reached for a less volatile topic. "When are you two scheduled to practice your routine for the parade?"

"I promised we'd do that tomorrow. He took time off from the GG for the days I'm here and he'd planned we'd hang out at the ranch together. Now that I've experienced ridin' he wants to go out with me."

"That sounds wonderful."

"Would you like to come with us?"

"Thanks, but I think not." She reached across the table and squeezed his arm. "I'm sure he's looking forward to hanging out with you."

"He did sound excited about that." He brightened. "We might come back to the GG tonight and catch Bryce and Nicole's show again."

"I'll be behind the bar."

"I know. I might have to keep goin' over there to order my beer."

"By all means. You're a good tipper."

He laughed. "Did I overplay my hand by givin' you that much?"

"I thought it was gallant. You covered my losses."

He chewed and swallowed his last bite of potato salad. "Not really. To do that I'd have had to give you a normal tip plus the ten. You were still in the hole."

"But that wouldn't have been as elegant. A single ten was perfect."

"Glad you thought so." He used his fork to point at his plate. "That was well tidy scran."

"Good food?"

"Aye."

"I should be writing all this down so I don't forget."

He grinned. "Keep me around and you won't have to."

Her heart constricted. "I would if I could."

"Ah, lass, I didn't—damn it to hell." He left his chair and pulled her from hers. "That was an idiot thing to say."

She reached up and smoothed her finger over the crease between his brows. "It's okay. This is a crazy situation we find ourselves in."

He drew her close. "Crazy and wonderful, all at the same time. You feel so good tucked in against me this way."

"You feel good, too."

"Will you come to bed with me, then?"

"Gladly."

"That's all I needed to hear." Without warning he swept her up in his arms, carried her the short distance and laid her gently on the rumpled coverlet.

The dashing move left her breathless. "Impressive."

"Always wanted to do that." He pulled out a condom before stripping off his jeans and briefs. "Figured you wouldn't mind."

"Mind?" She wiggled out of her cover-up and tossed it aside. "I found it highly romantic."

"Good, because that's the way it was meant." He rolled on the condom and climbed into bed with her. "And I'm hopin' you'll forgive me if we move straight to the main event, because...I ache to be inside you."

"Nothing to forgive." She welcomed him into her arms. "I ache to have you there."

"Truly?" He braced himself above her.

She smiled. "Truly." Sliding her hands down his muscled back, she cupped his taut backside. "Feeling your tadger buried deep inside me is pure barry."

His green eyes sparkled with delight. "I've never heard sweeter words in my entire life."

"Should I embroider them on a pillow for you?"

"Aye, do that." He entered her slowly, his gaze intent on her face. "And make another that says *feeling my tadger sink into your warm sheath is pure barry.*"

"One for each side of the bed." The slow glide set off tiny explosions deep in her core. She'd come in no time at all.

"When others are around..." He paused to suck in air. "We can turn them to the opposite side where you've embroidered..." He groaned softly as he completed the maneuver and locked in tight. "Lovely flowers."

"Right." Her pulse raced and her body quivered. "Only thing is...I can't embroider."

He gave her a lopsided grin. "Could take a while then."

"But this won't." She gulped. "I'm close."

"Right there with you." Leaning down, he feathered a kiss over her mouth. "If we stay very still, we might be able to hold off."

"Where's the...fun in that?"

"I have no idea." He lifted his head and met her gaze. "Wrap your arms around my back and your legs around my hips."

"Done."

He eased his tadger back almost to her entrance and slipped one hand under her hip. "Hang on."

His first vigorous thrust lifted her off the bed. But he steadied her with his hand at her hip while balancing his weight on the other. She barely had time to marvel at the strength that required before he took her on a thrill ride that quickly brought her one climax, then another and *another.*

He drove home one last time before he gasped and shuddered in the grip of his release. Chest heaving, he fought for each breath. She held on tight. Gradually his breathing calmed and he lowered her, trembling, to the bed.

He bowed his head. As sweat from his brow fell like warm rain on her heaving breasts, he murmured a phrase in an unfamiliar language.

Then he drew in a ragged breath and looked up. His hair clung in tendrils to his damp forehead and he gazed at her through lashes spiked with moisture. "Thank you, lass."

"I loved every single second."

"I'm glad."

"What was that language?"

"Gaelic."

"What were you saying?"

His smile was tender as he slowly shook his head. But the answer was there in his eyes.

<u>22</u>

Ta gra agam duit. I love you. Saying it in Gaelic was a cheat, but Aleck didn't care. Tansy hadn't pressed him for the meaning, which told him she'd guessed it.

Although he was confused about many things regarding this unexpected turn his life had taken, he wasn't confused about his feelings for her. Even if a few intense hours were all they'd ever have, that didn't change the depth of emotion lodged permanently in his heart.

He was in her wee bathroom disposing of the condom when she called to him. He had a message on his phone. Rory, no doubt.

When he came out, she was sitting on the edge of the bed and she'd put on that filmy thing that revealed more than it concealed. Guaranteed to work him into a lather. He didn't mind. He'd never been more alive than when his body craved hers.

She handed him his phone. "I'll bet the road's dry enough."

"Could be." He tapped on the message. "It is. He can bring your truck in and it needs to be before five. Zane and Mandy are back in their own house, and the Sawyer clan is gatherin' at the ranch for a cook-out tonight so they can meet me. Might be some others there, too."

"Tell him to go ahead and come now."

His gaze found hers. "You kickin' me out, lass?"

She smiled. "I've had you long enough. We've been together for almost twenty-four hours."

"But some of those hours we were sleepin'!"

"Even so, considering your short visit, I've already appropriated a large part of it. I'll feel a whole lot better if Rory picks you up and takes you back to the ranch. He wants to show you off to Quinn's family and their other friends. He's so proud of you, Aleck."

"Probably means we won't be drivin' in for Bryce and Nicole's show." Which he wanted to see again, but mostly it was an excuse to have some contact with Tansy, even if she was working.

"You likely won't come in tonight, but Kendra wants to see it. You can lobby for tomorrow night."

"I won't be seein' you until tomorrow *night*?"

"That's not so far away."

"I beg to differ. I feel as if I've lived a lifetime in these past twenty-four hours. Time is relative."

Amusement flickered in her eyes. "I've heard that somewhere."

"All I'm sayin' is that tomorrow night seems like a lifetime from now."

She just looked at him like he was a bampot. And for good reason. He was complaining about not seeing her for one whole day and night, but he'd fly out of here on Friday and no telling when they'd lay eyes on each other again.

He scrubbed a hand through his still-damp hair. 'I'm not makin' any sense, am I?"

"No, but feel free to rave on as much as you want. I love hearing you talk."

He sighed as resignation set in. "You have the right of it. I want to meet Quinn's family and spend more time with Rory. That is why I'm here." He gazed at her. "I just didn't figure on you."

"Are you sorry?"

"Nay! Never that! You're the most amazin' woman I've ever..." He trailed off. Better stop before he said more than he should. "I'll text Rory. And if I may, I'd like to use your wee shower."

"You may." She had that glow in her eyes again, the one that told him he wasn't the only one in this pickle.

"Thank you." He quickly texted Rory and laid the phone on the narrow dresser she had near the bathroom door. A cold shower might help cool him off.

Then he paused and glanced at Tansy. "I wasn't thinkin'. If you're comin' downstairs with me when Rory brings the truck, you might want a shower. You can be first."

"No, you go ahead. I'll grab one after you're done. It's more important that you're ready."

Once again, she was right. "I'll make it quick." He did his best to hurry, which wasn't easy in such a wee space. He banged into the shower walls at least a dozen times. On top of that, he was on sensual overload because the soap and shampoo inspired hot images of making love to her.

Eventually he stepped out, elbows smarting and tadger agitated. He grabbed the towel hanging nearby and began drying off, taunted by her scent clinging to the terrycloth.

He couldn't identify the aroma precisely, didn't need to. It was simply *Au de Tansy*. And that was enough to create a yearning nearly impossible to resist.

Once he was no longer dripping, he came out of the bathroom still drying his wet hair. Judging from the sound of water running and the clatter of silverware, she was in the kitchen messing with dishes. The noise level had increased downstairs, too. The afternoon lull must be over.

He raised his voice. "I took the bath towel you had in there. Do you need it?"

"I have a spare."

"That's good because this one is damp. But I'm finished, if you want to jump in the shower."

"Thanks, I will." She came out of the kitchen area, walked toward him and leaned down to open the bottom drawer of the small dresser. "This apartment is a little like the cabin of a cruise ship. I can't be overstocked on anything that takes up room, which can be a pain, but—"

"I don't want to go."

She glanced up. "You mean now? Or—"

"Friday." He took a breath. "But I will."

Towel clutched to her chest, she stood. "I'm prepared for that."

"I'm not. And thinkin' about it is turnin' me into a bampot."

"A bampot?"

"An idiot."

"You're not—"

"I am, lass. It's good that Rory's pickin' me up. I'll work on myself between now and tomorrow night. I'll do better, Tansy-girl."

The glow returned to her eyes. "No one's ever called me that." Her voice was soft as a caress. "I like it."

"Good." He held her gaze for as long as he dared. When the urge to kiss her threatened to destroy his judgment, he turned away. "We need to get movin'."

She smiled. "Aye."

His heart squeezed. Every time she spoke a Scottish word she forged another tender link between them. How strong would it become? Would it stretch all the way across the Atlantic?

He dressed quickly. Wild Creek wasn't far away. Rory would be pulling in soon. He was putting on his boots when Tansy came out of the shower, her hair pinned on top of her head and a towel around her delicious body.

Because the bathroom was so wee, she'd have to dress right in front of him. He couldn't handle that without cracking. "I'll head downstairs to wait." He stood and grabbed his phone from the dresser.

"Good idea. Tell Rory the keys are under the seat."

"I will, lass." Taking his hat from the knob, he put it on and opened the door, letting in the noise from below. "See you in a bit." Kissing her would be a mistake so he touched two fingers to the brim of his hat the way Rory did whenever he left Damaris.

"See you soon, cowboy." Her voice sounded funny, like she had a cold.

He took the stairs two at a time, relieved that the GG was so busy. Helped him make it out the back door without either Michael or Bryce stopping him. He wasn't in the mood for a blether with either of them.

No sooner had he stepped outside than the purple nose of Tansy's wee truck rounded the corner of the building. Aleck gave Rory a wave and he lightly tapped the horn.

Cruising past Aleck, he swung around and neatly backed into a spot on the far side of the door. The lad had become an expert at driving American style. Aleck went to meet him.

"Hey, big brother!" Rory climbed out and shut the door. "I guess Tansy wouldn't loan you her razor."

"She likes the fluff."

Rory's eyebrows lifted. "Does she, now?" He cocked his head this way and that. "Does add to the gravitas. Just don't remember ever seein' you with fluff before."

"I'll shave it before I go in on Saturday. Wouldn't sit right with Campbell."

"You're still leavin', then?"

"Aye."

Rory held his gaze. "How'd it go?"

Pure barry. "Good. It went good."

"Better'n that judgin' from the gleam in your eye."

Aleck ducked his head, afraid his brother would see too much. "She's a bonnie lass."

"You're not tellin' me anythin' new. O' course she's bonnie. But is she as special as you—"

The back door opened.

Rory cleared his throat. "Personally I think it would be special if we played for the folks." He turned toward the building. "Hey, Tansy! Wish you didn't have to work tonight so you could come out to the ranch."

"No worries." She walked toward them wearing shorts and a t-shirt. Her hair was still in a loose arrangement on top of her head. Clearly she hadn't dressed for work yet. She shaded her eyes against the sun. "So you and Aleck will play for the group tonight?"

"If Aleck is willin'."

"Sure. The more we play together the better."

"Aunt Kendra loves the idea. She wants one of her boys to learn the pipes."

"Yeah?" Aleck smiled. Evidently his playing was a hit. "Any takers?"

"Zane's willin' but doesn't feel he has the time, especially now. None of the others are ready to tackle it. Badger's up for it, though."

"Who's Badger?"

Tansy grinned. "Thaddeus Livingston Calhoun the Third, who prefers to be called Badger."

"So would I," Aleck said. "Scottish, is he?"

"Has kinfolk from there," Rory said. "Never thought much about his roots until recently. Now he's into it, researchin' tartans and crests. He and Hayley, that's his sweetheart, just started watchin' *Outlander* with Damaris and me."

"Why does the name Badger sound familiar?"

"He's co-owner of—"

"Badger Air." Aleck finally put it together. "Couldn't remember where I'd heard that name before."

"He'll be there tonight. He's kind of an honorary member of the family." Rory glanced at Tansy. "Sure you can't make it?"

"I'm afraid not. I promised Michael I'd work the next three nights. He's counting on me. And thank you, by the way, for driving my truck in."

"Happy to do it. Thanks to your rescue effort, Damaris put in some quality time on her laptop today and I was able to help clean up after the storm."

"Good. How's the road?"

"Bumpy as hell, and you have to drive around some of the deeper puddles, but it's doable, especially in a bigger rig like mine. I had to be careful with your wee truck, but it should be better by around noon tomorrow if you want to come out."

"Thanks for the update, but I wasn't planning on it."

"Why not?"

"I...have several chores I should take care of."

"She doesn't want to intrude," Aleck said.

"*Intrude?*" Rory stared at Tansy in confusion. "How could you think you'd be—"

"I've sort of monopolized him since yesterday. He came to see you, and so I wanted you two to have some time together without me."

Rory glanced at him. "And you're fine with that?"

He shrugged. "I guess she has a point."

Taking off his hat, Rory scrubbed a hand through his ginger hair. "I can see you're tryin' to be considerate, lass, but if you'll pardon me sayin' so, your head's full o' mince."

"You think I'm crazy?"

"Aye, I do, no insult intended. After all you went through to get this brother of mine alone for a couple of hours, why give up the chance to see him during the day tomorrow? He's leavin' on Friday, y'know."

"I do know. But wouldn't you like to have some bro time with him?"

"Sure I would, but I was figuring on includin' Damaris in whatever we do. He came as much to see her as he did to see me. It's not like Aleck and I will go off by ourselves and swap stories we wouldn't want ladies to hear. That's not how we roll. Am I right, big brother?"

"Aye." He glanced at her. "I do want you out there, lass. I promise to be fit company if you'll consider it."

"You been causin' trouble?"

"No, he hasn't." Tansy smiled. "He just doesn't like the idea that he has to leave on Friday. It makes him a bit...erratic."

"I know exactly how to fix that." Rory gave him a look that said he was up to something. "Come out around noon, lass. He'll be in fine shape by then."

She laughed. "How can I resist an invitation like that?"

"Then you'll drive out?" Aleck didn't much care what Rory had in store for him if it meant he'd get to see Tansy tomorrow.

"I will."

"Excellent."

Rory gazed at them and nodded. "That's better. Got some keys for me, lass?"

"They're under the seat."

"Didn't get around to tellin' him." Too busy covering up the heart I'm wearing on my sleeve.

"We'd better shove off, then. Need to decide on a set list if we're goin' to perform tonight."

"Right."

"See you tomorrow, Tansy." Rory touched the brim of his hat and started around to the driver's side of his truck.

Aleck gave himself a few more precious seconds. She wore rubber thongs on her feet. And there were those multi-colored toes. He loved her so much his chest hurt. He closed the distance between them and gave her a quick kiss. "I'm glad you're comin' out to the ranch tomorrow."

"Me, too."

He strode to the truck, which was already running, and climbed in.

Rory took his foot off the brake. "Glad to see you kiss her. Beginnin' to think you two had a fight or somethin'." He pulled out and drove down the back alley that led to the street. "What erratic nonsense were you up to?"

"Stupid stuff." Aleck looked in the side view mirror and she was still there, shading her eyes against the sun, watching them leave. Then they rounded the building and he couldn't see her anymore. His stomach hollowed out. He missed her already.

"You're in love with her."

He let out a gusty sigh. "I am."

"Then why did you agree with her plan to stay away from you tomorrow?"

"Because I'm in love with her."

"Huh?"

"I don't know what the hell to do. I can't imagine leavin' on Friday but I can't stay, either. It's tearin' me up inside and I thought she might need a break from me."

"Clearly she doesn't."

"Guess not. Oh, and by the way, she's in love with me, too."

"Did she say that?"

"No, but I know she is. I didn't say it to her, either, at least not in English."

"What then? Swahili?"

Aleck snorted. "Gaelic."

"Oh, because that isn't weird."

"It didn't feel weird at the time."

"Not to *you*, the bampot who took it into his head to start spoutin' Gaelic."

He choked on a laugh. Okay, so it was funny.

"No wonder she suggested not comin' out to the ranch tomorrow. Did she recommend you see someone?"

"No." He grinned. When his brother got on a roll, there was no stopping him. "I'm sure she knew what I was up to and I guess she thought it made some kind of idiotic sense."

"Idiotic is right. I know you took it in school and you're proud of it and all, but that doesn't mean you should start throwin' out phrases helter-skelter. It's not like French or Spanish. You'll freak people out."

"She wasn't freaked out. I'll bet she's lookin' up *I love you* in Gaelic on her phone right now."

"Or she's lookin' up warnin' signs of aberrant behavior to find out what kind of kook she's mixed up with."

That did it. He laughed until the tears came. When he could talk again, he glanced at his brother. "Thanks, Rory."

"For what?"

"For fixin' what I messed up. And makin' me laugh about it."

"You're welcome. For a minute there I thought you were takin' yourself seriously."

"I sometimes have a problem with that."

"Really? I hadn't noticed."

"What's your evil plan for gettin' me straightened out before she shows up tomorrow?"

Rory chuckled. "You'll find out."

23

Thanks to Rory helping him find his lost sense of humor, Aleck had a great time at the cookout. Steaks grilled over an open fire, more side dishes than he had time to sample and plenty of beer made for well tidy scran.

Damaris and Rory stuck close to make sure he met everyone. He did a fair job of keeping them all straight now that he wasn't jetlagged, even though nearly everyone there was new except Quinn, Aunt Kendra, Brendan and Jo.

Toward the end of the meal, Gage and Emma's little boy, Josh, started making the rounds of the grownups. The fair-haired toddler had everyone in the palm of his chubby hand. He took full advantage of it, moving from one doting relative to the next. His newlywed parents looked on with a smile.

Rory got up. "Another beer before our gig? Keep you nice and relaxed during the performance."

Damaris peered at him. "Are you nervous? You don't look nervous."

"I'm not, but I wouldn't object to another beer." He loved being around these two. They were so comfortable with each other. Reminded him of his ma and da.

"Three beers, comin' up." Rory took off in the direction of the claw-foot bathtub filled with ice that served as a beverage cooler.

"How're you guys doing?" Aunt Kendra left her spot and perched on the section of bench Rory had just vacated.

"Great." Aleck gestured to the picnic area. "What a bonnie setup."

"I love it, especially this time of year. Have you had a chance to talk to Badger?"

"Not long. Got introduced, but that's about it. He's from the South, right?"

"Atlanta. He's excited about learning the pipes. He saw the video Ryker took of you playing *When a Child is Born*."

"Ryker took a video? I didn't know that."

"He did his best to be subtle. Didn't want to throw you off. He showed it to Badger today and now Badger wants to serenade Hayley with a bagpipe tune at their wedding."

"When's the wedding?"

"September."

"*This* September?"

"Uh-huh."

"I'd hate to discourage him, but that's not much time."

"Much time for what?" Rory came over and handed him a beer. "Can I get you somethin', Aunt Kendra?"

She glanced up. "No thanks. I took your seat."

"Keep it. I need to stretch my legs, anyway. Who's runnin' out of time? Besides my brother, o' course."

"Badger. He wants to be able to play the pipes for the wedding."

"In September?" Rory shook his head. "He's a determined guy, but—"

"Maybe somethin' simple." Aleck sipped his beer. A couple of his earliest pieces were appropriate and might work. "He'd have to practice a lot between now and then."

"It's not impossible," Rory said. "Nothin' is, but still. I wonder if he's told Luke about this plan. It's not just his and Hayley's wedding, but Luke and Abigail's, too."

"A double weddin'?"

"Oh, yes." Kendra grinned. "Virginia, Hayley and Luke's mom, has been dreaming about this double wedding for more than a year. The kids have been dragging their feet. They finally all agreed to it, and she's ecstatic."

"Isn't she a weddin' planner?"

"Listen to you, Aleck McGavin." Damaris gave him a friendly nudge. "With that recall, someone might mistake you for a lawyer."

He chuckled. "That they might." He took another swallow of his beer and turned to Kendra. "When do you want Rory and me to play?"

"Anytime you're ready. Looks like everyone's about finished with dinner. Soon Josh will need something to distract him."

"He sure is sociable."

"Yep. I should warn you he brought his kazoo. He takes it everywhere and will likely be inspired to play when he sees you perform. But he's not very loud."

"I'll drown out that wee lad I'm afraid. Maybe we can invite him to play when it's just Rory drummin'. Rory can soften his sound better than I can."

"See how it goes. And maybe you'll have a chance to talk with Badger when you're done."

"I'll make certain of it." He finished off his beer and glanced at Rory. "Showtime."

After they brought their instruments out to the picnic area, Aunt Kendra gave them a brief introduction. They'd decided to save their tartan gear for the parade. Aleck had figured out how to play while wearing his Stetson, so Rory wore his.

Right before they started, Rory looked over at him. "A cowboy on the pipes. Looks better'n I thought it would."

"You don't look so bad, yourself." He grinned. *"Craic mhaith, laddie."* He started tapping his foot.

His brother rolled his eyes. "Won't even ask."

"Good times, Rory. Good times." And they were off, making music together again, playing to an enthusiastic audience that whooped and hollered at the end of each number.

Aleck invited Josh up midway through the set, and the little boy rocked out on his kazoo, accompanied quietly by Rory. He could make those sticks whisper when he chose to.

Naturally the little guy didn't want to leave the limelight. Rather than reduce the kid to tears, Aleck let him stay. Josh didn't seem to mind that his efforts on the kazoo were obliterated by the commanding sound of the Highland Pipes.

They finished up with the *Skye Boat Song* for Damaris's sake, but several other lasses in the group became dreamy-eyed over that tune. Judging from the response at the end of the set, they'd met expectations.

Aunt Kendra hurried up to thank them, followed by the entire Sawyer contingent. Emma and Gage couldn't say enough nice things about the thrill they'd given Josh.

High on the energy of the crowd, Aleck turned to his brother. "That *Skye Boat Song*? The lasses love it. We should keep it in."

Rory smiled. "You mean for all the other times we perform in this town?"

He blinked. "Sorry. Took a wee trip down memory lane."

"Not that I wouldn't love you to bring the pipes over each time you visit, but—"

"Totally impractical." He laid them on the nearest vacant picnic table.

"That was amazin'!"

Southern accent. Aleck turned and held out his hand. "Badger, right?"

"Hey, good memory."

"Need one around here."

"No kiddin'. This is my fiancée, Hayley Bennett."

"Pleased to meet you." Hayley was nearly as tall as he was.

"Same here. I especially loved the theme from *Outlander.* Badger and I are watching it with Rory and Damaris."

"So I heard."

Badger eyed the pipes lying on the table. "Kendra said she told you I was interested in learnin' how to play."

"She did. It's a great instrument. Lots of history behind it."

Badger nodded. "Been researchin'. Really want to learn how to play."

"I'd be glad to give you a few tips to get you started."

"That would make me happier than a pig frog in the Okefenokee Swamp."

Aleck smiled. "Is that good?"

"Very good. Pig frogs rock. That's what I'm comin' back as."

Hayley laughed. "Then you'd better enjoy our life together in our current incarnation, because this chick isn't coming back as a pig frog."

"That's what you think, darlin'. You'll want to once you know more. But we're gettin' off the subject. Tell me, Aleck. How long will it take me to learn to play? I mean, so I can perform a tune at our wedding."

"Aunt Kendra said you're gettin' married in September."

"Yessir, September fourteenth, under a Harvest Moon."

"Nice."

"We think so. Anyway, I've been diggin' into my Scottish background and when Rory showed me that video, I got it into my head that I want to play somethin' as part of the ceremony."

Aleck gazed at him. "How disciplined are you?"

"Are you talking about my protégé?" Quinn joined the group. "Because I can vouch for Badger's dedication when he wants to learn something new. He took up scratchboard art last year and he's already selling it."

Badger smiled. "Thank you kindly, Quinn. But I seem to have some talent for that. No tellin' if I have any talent for this."

"One way to find out," Aleck said. "Give it a try. I'll steer you in the right direction. We can text, or do video chats, whatever works for you."

"I appreciate that. I wish you weren't leavin' so soon, though. I think one of the reasons I learned scratchboard art so fast is face-to-face lessons with Quinn."

"Believe me, I'd love to stay longer." Understatement of the year. "Maybe you can find someone around here who'd give you that kind of help."

"I might. But there's something special about learnin' from a family member."

Family member? Badger wasn't related to him or Quinn...oh, wait. Rory had said Badger was just like family.

"I can see I confused you with that statement," Badger said. "The thing is, I'm a heck of a lot closer to the McGavins, the Sawyers, and the Bennetts than I am to my folks."

And clearly the affection was mutual. Aleck nodded. "I'd be here for you if I could."

"In any case, you'll come for the weddin', I hope."

"Well, I—"

"Worst case scenario, if I can't play a decent tune, I'd love to have you do it. I want bagpipes at this weddin', come hell or high water. I'd be happy to pay to fly you out if you'll come."

"But didn't you just see that video this mornin'?"

"That's a fact. It was love at first sight between me and those pipes, just like I fell for Hayley the minute I laid eyes on her. Don't know if you've ever experienced that."

What had Badger heard? Judging from his steady gaze, he knew about Tansy. "Aye." He took a deep breath. "I definitely have."

"So you'll come to the weddin'?"

"I'll call my boss in the mornin' and see if I can take vacation time."

Rory gripped his shoulder and squeezed. "Well done."

24

Tansy took the ranch road at a snail's pace to protect her truck's shocks. Good thing she'd started out early. Not that starting early had been a problem. She'd been awake and ready to go at dawn, but she wasn't expected until noon so she'd spent a restless morning.

Aleck had texted her not to eat lunch because they were packing one to take on the trail. She couldn't wait. Coming out here to go riding with Rory and Damaris was a comforting and familiar routine. Adding Aleck to the mix turned it into a celebratory event.

When she reached the end of the road, she glanced toward the barn where Jim Underwood was moving among four saddled horses tied to the hitching post. The lanky foreman waved and she tooted her horn.

Might as well park down by the barn. Whenever she rode with Rory and Damaris, they took Jake, Diablo and Strawberry. Winston had been added to the mix, probably for Rory since he'd want Aleck to ride Diablo.

As she parked near the barn, Jim went back inside. A few seconds later, Aleck came out, his stride brisk and his grin a mile wide. Her skin flushed with happiness and she smiled back. *Thank you, Rory.*

He rounded the nose of her truck and opened her door. "It's good to see you, lass."

"It's good to see you, too." She left her hat on the seat and climbed out. He held his ground, very much in her space. She didn't mind. So what if she had some trouble getting her breath? "Your beard's growing in nicely. There's a bit of red to it."

He nudged back his hat. "One kiss, here by the truck. That'll have to do for now."

"Are they ready to go?"

"They're up at the house fetchin' our lunch. I asked if I could stay down here and meet you. I'm sure they know why. Will your lipstick smear?"

She rested her palms on his warm chest. "Probably."

"Did you bring more or do I have to be careful?"

"*Can* you be careful? As I recall, you're a very lusty—"

"I can do anything that's required if it means I get a wee kiss."

"You're funny."

"And you're the bonniest lass I've ever known." Cupping her shoulders, he held her fast and dipped his head. "Must I be careful?"

"I brought lipstick."

"Good thinkin'." He covered her mouth with his.

Heaven help her, she caught fire instantly. Gripping the back of his head with both hands, she opened to him, pulling him deeper into the kiss and welcoming the firm thrust of his tongue.

His breath roughened and his fingers tightened on her shoulders as he made sweet love to her mouth. She whimpered, longing to snuggle against him, but he held her firmly, not allowing their bodies to touch.

Much too soon, he drew back, gasping. "Your mouth is…temptation enough, lass. If I hold you any closer…" His hot gaze said it all.

She gulped and nodded. "Understood."

"I feel obliged to mention that we have no plan goin' forward."

"No, we don't." She dragged in a breath. "What do you think?"

"We're all comin' into town tonight for the show. Rory wondered if I wanted to be left there with you."

Her pulse raced. "What did you tell him?"

"I said I'd ask if—"

"Silly man! Yes!"

His gaze sparkled. "Alrighty, then. It's a date. I'll be bringin' my tartan."

"You'll dress for the parade at my place?"

"Makes the most sense. Rory will transport my pipes, but I need to be dressed and ready to go when he gets there."

"I'm really excited, now."

His eyebrows lifted. "More excited about my plaid than my tadger, are you?"

She laughed. "I've experienced the one, but I've never watched a Scotsman suit up. That could be extremely—"

"Hey, you two lovebirds!" Rory's voice rang out. "Wrap it up! Winston's gettin' impatient!"

The Paint whinnied obligingly.

"See? Don't want to keep that horse waitin'!"

"Be there in a minute!" Aleck examined her mouth. "You need fixin'." He pulled a red bandana out of his back pocket and began carefully wiping the area around her lips.

"Where did you get a bandana?"

"Rory gave me several of his. Already used one this mornin' while I was muckin' out stalls. Came in handy."

"You cleaned stalls?"

"Aye. Worked with Rory and Jim Underwood. Great guy." He smiled and stepped back. "Better put on a wee bit more. I kissed most of it off."

"Okay." She grabbed her lipstick out of her purse and used her side view mirror to put it on. "Nice of you to help clean stalls." She recapped the tube and stuck it back in her purse.

"Didn't do it to be nice."

"Oh?" Retrieving her hat, she shut the door and turned to him. "Then why?"

He grinned. "My brother said it was good for what ails me."

"And was it?"

He glanced at her. "Absolutely."

"What did—"

"Tell you about it later."

***

Tansy willingly tabled her questions now that she'd have private time with Aleck tonight. Whatever his insights, they'd clearly put him in a cheerful mood. He laughed and joked with Damaris and Rory as everyone mounted up.

Damaris had grown up riding the trails at Wild Creek, so she took the lead on Jake as they headed out, followed by Rory on Winston. Tansy was the second most experienced rider, so she and Strawberry brought up the rear, following behind Aleck on Diablo.

He was learning fast. His heels stayed down and he seldom gripped the saddle horn anymore. His neck reining abilities had improved, too. Considering this was only the second horseback ride of his life, he was doing great.

Rory turned in the saddle to grin at Aleck. "Tickles me to see you moseyin' down the trail behind me, big brother."

"Tickles me to hear you use the word *mosey*. Next thing I know you'll be chewin' on a piece of straw and sayin' *I reckon it'll rain tonight*."

"I already say that. Damaris, didn't I just say that?"

"No, you said *the night's pure dreich* like you always do. Makes me giggle."

"I love the Scottish phrases," Tansy said. "They're so colorful. I hope you hang onto them, Rory."

"Damaris says that, too. Havin' Aleck around helps. Did he tell you he might be comin' back for the weddin' in September?"

"No, he didn't." Talk about a conversational bombshell.

"Guess he was too busy kissin' to mention it."

Aleck looked over his shoulder. "I was plannin' to tell you, lass."

"No worries."

"I still need to check with Campbell. He wasn't in when I called this mornin' so I'll try again tomorrow mornin' before the parade."

"Sounds good." Could he tell that inside she was dancing a jig at the possibility that he was even considering it?

"Badger wants Aleck to be his backup in case he can't learn the pipes fast enough to play at his weddin'."

"That was his plan? I don't know a whole lot about bagpipes, but is that even possible?"

"Might be," Aleck said. "I'm convinced he'll work really hard, but it wouldn't hurt to have me as backup if it doesn't come together for him."

"It would make it easier to think of you leaving if you're coming back in a couple of months." Did she sound giddy?

Must have, because he gripped the pommel and turned to give her a smile. "Was hopin' you'd be excited about the idea."

"I certainly am."

"Me, too."

"How's everyone doing?" Damaris took advantage of a curve in the trail to stop and glance back. "Specifically, how are you doing, Aleck?"

"Unless I start takin' videos and forget I'm seated on a horse, I'll be fine."

"I doubt you'd make that same mistake twice. We'll go another mile or so down the trail and stop."

"Assumin' I work it out to come back in September, will I have lost the ground I've gained?"

"Probably not, but it wouldn't hurt if you do some riding when you get home. Is there a stable in your area?"

"Don't know. Never mattered before. I'll check it out."

"I'll bet there is." Rory beamed at him. "Like she said, it would keep you in the habit of ridin'. Next time I'll show you the spot where Zane releases his birds."

"And if you're lucky," Damaris said, "he might be releasing one while you're here. If he knows you're coming, he might be able to make that happen."

"I can't believe I haven't done that yet," Tansy said. "I so wanted to go with you guys last month but then Michael got the flu..."

"That was tough luck," Damaris said. "Next time."

"Zane takes them on a horse? I can't imagine how he—"

"They're in a carrier." Rory gestured toward Jake. "He rides this horse because he's used to havin' the carrier on his back."

"So I was on Strawberry that day," Damaris said. "We rode out to the edge of a ravine where there's always a nice updraft, which helps the bird gain momentum."

"Spectacular experience, seein' that bald eagle take flight." Rory took a breath. "I'm not ashamed to say it brought tears to my eyes."

"I'd love bein' a part of that." Aleck glanced at her. "A lot of variables, though."

And he wasn't comfortable with variables. She gave him a smile of encouragement. "Let's hope it works out."

"We'll think positive," Damaris said. "Let's get going, okay? I'm hungry." She clucked to her horse and started back down the trail.

Aleck might be coming back in *two months*. No guarantee, but what an improvement over having him leave with no specific plan to return. Maybe they'd go to the wedding together. He might even end up playing his pipes if Badger's skills weren't up to snuff.

Which brought up another issue. "Hey, Aleck, are you taking your pipes home or leaving them here?"

He looked over his shoulder. "Been thinkin' about that. The pipe band doesn't have any gigs scheduled between now and then. August is usually slow for us. If Campbell gives me the time off, it would be easier to leave them here."

"Damaris and I can keep 'em," Rory said. "Or maybe Aunt Kendra could."

"I'm sure she'd be willin'," Aleck said, "but I'd feel better if you had them, Rory. I know you have a wee cabin, but—"

"I get it." Rory said. "We'll keep 'em for you."

"Or I could take them." It was a bold statement that assumed she had girlfriend status and could be trusted with something that valuable. Clearly he treasured those pipes.

"That's an idea," Aleck said. "You know what? Now that I've seen your place, I think you might actually have more room for them."

"Then she should definitely take them." Rory didn't hesitate. "I confess Damaris and I are a wee bit crunched in that cabin. Come to think of it, you might have more square footage and storage possibilities than we do, Tansy."

"I think I do. So it's decided. If Campbell gives you the go ahead, then after the parade, you can store them with me until September."

Having him come back then would be lovely. It made the ocean that still separated them seem a little smaller.

<u>**25**</u>

"Now, because you're so responsible, I'm not too worried, but you need to be ready when I get there in the mornin'." Rory had to raise his voice to be heard over the country band that had followed Bryce and Nicole's show.

"I'll be ready." Aleck appreciated that Rory and Damaris had stayed to keep him company after the rest of the family had left, but he'd rather not talk about tomorrow. He was far more focused on the present. Tansy got off work in about thirty minutes. He'd carried a duffle loaded with his tartan up to her apartment when he'd arrived.

"I don't expect you to be rested. Just ready."

Aleck chuckled. "Wise man."

"Damaris and I will be waitin' in the parkin' lot at six sharp. That should give us enough time to walk down to the stagin' area and check in when we're supposed to. Want me to text you when we leave the ranch?"

"No. I'll be ready."

"Alrighty, then. I'm glad you're doin' this parade with me, for a lot of reasons, but if we didn't have this gig, I'd be ridin' on the GG float tomorrow jugglin' servin' trays."

"The GG has a float?"

"Aye, and marchin' is way more my style than ridin' on a float."

"Why would you be jugglin' trays?"

"They didn't have a bear suit to fit me. They had one to fit Tansy, though."

"She's wearin' a bear suit tomorrow?"

"She didn't tell you?"

Maybe he did need to hear about tomorrow, after all. "No, she—"

"Never mind. You guys have been busy with other things. She's wearin' a suit Aunt Kendra loaned her from a previous event. Unless you knew it was her, you wouldn't recognize her. She'll be dancin' around while Nicole and Bryce play."

"Then I guess she'll be walkin' down with us."

"That's what I figured."

"She was probably goin' to tell me tonight."

"Probably." Rory smiled. "Unless you get distracted."

"Aye." Anticipation churned in his gut.

Damaris leaned around Rory. "I'll be wearing a pygmy owl costume tomorrow."

"Why?"

"I'm riding on the Raptors Rise float. The Whine and Cheese Club is short one of their members because Judy's out of town, so—" She paused. "You have no idea what I'm talking about, do you?"

"I have some idea, lass. Rory mentioned the Whine and Cheese ladies. Aunt Kendra and Jo are members, but why are they on the Raptors Rise float?"

"Since the baby was due any day, Kendra and Jo volunteered the Whine and Cheese Club to handle their float this year. They're huge backers of the sanctuary so it makes sense."

"And you'll be a pygmy owl?"

"Right. That's Judy's costume. I'm taller than she is but I'll make it work. Mandy created the outfits a year ago. She didn't finish in time for the parade, so they used them for a Raptors Rise benefit later. They deserve another outing, though."

"They sure do," Rory said. "I've seen Aunt Kendra's, which is a golden eagle. Jo's a falcon, Christine's a bald eagle and Deidre's a barn owl. I haven't seen those other three, but I'm sure they're amazin', too. They should be in the parade every year."

"I had no idea this thing would be so elaborate."

"And fun." Damaris grinned. "We're dancing to *Shake Ya Tailfeather.*"

Aleck frowned. "I don't know that one."

"I didn't either," Rory said. "But it's cute. When they sing the chorus, they turn around and shake their bums. I hate that we won't see it but we're also a musical entry so they can't have two together. Even if you weren't here, I wouldn't have seen it because I'd be on the GG float jugglin'."

"Can you juggle?"

"I can, now. Cody taught me. He learned it from Badger and Ryker, who taught themselves when they were in the military. They've already recruited me for the Christmas show. I think Raven juggles, too."

"Christmas show?"

"Yeah, they have it here, in the GG. It's a local talent show and proceeds go to Eagles Nest families in need. I hear that it's great fun."

"I'm sure it is."

"You know what? You should come over for that. We should get Ma and Da to make the trip, too." He turned to Damaris. "How about it, lass? Would that be pure tidy, havin' everyone here for Christmas?"

"Sure would." She leaned over and gave him a quick kiss on the cheek. "What do you say, Aleck?"

"My head is spinnin'. I'll have to see. I've told Badger I'd try to make it to his weddin'. If that works out the way we hope, then comin' again in December...that's a lot of days away. I don't think Campbell will go for it."

Rory held his gaze. "Then I guess you'd have to quit." His tone was casual, but he wasn't smiling the way he did when he was making a joke.

Aleck sucked in a breath. "I—"

"Oh, listen to that! They're playing our song. Come dance with me." Damaris got up and tugged on his arm.

"What do you mean, lass? That's not our—"

"Dance with me, Rory McGavin, and leave poor Aleck alone."

"Aye." He got up. "Sorry, big brother. Sometimes I get carried away."

After they left, he exhaled slowly. He still had beer in his mug but he didn't pick it up.

Instead he turned in his chair so he had a better view of the bar. Last call had gone out a while ago, so Tansy wasn't serving anymore.

Instead she was having a blether with Michael while the two of them shared the cleanup routine, polishing mugs and stacking them in a pyramid along the mirrored back of the antique bar. They both wore black logo t-shirts and matching black Stetsons, the GG uniform.

He wore it, as well. While he'd been mucking out stalls, Kendra had washed some of his stuff, including the t-shirt. He'd found it lying on his bed when he'd come back to his room after taking a shower this afternoon.

She'd left a note—*We're all wearing our shirts tonight. It's a McGavin thing. Welcome to the tribe.* Tansy wasn't related, but clearly she was part of that tribe. Like Badger, she'd found a more solid connection here than with the family she'd been born into.

That cast a whole new light on the plan he'd concocted this morning after shoveling horse apples for a couple of hours. At the time, it had seemed like the way to go. He'd figured they'd talk about it tonight, after they'd made love. She might have said yes, although probably not if she was smart.

Rory and Damaris returned from the dance floor and remained standing.

"We're goin' to shove off," Rory said.

Aleck got to his feet. "Thanks for stayin'. You know how I hate to drink alone."

"Thanks for buyin'." His brother's chest heaved. "Listen, I apologize for sayin' what I did. As Damaris has rightly pointed out, it's not my place."

"In his defense, he only says things like that because he loves you." Damaris's gaze was warm. "So do I, Aleck. I can't tell you how much it's meant to me, getting to know you."

"Same here." He gave her a hug. "I don't know if that Christmas thing will happen, but Ma and Da will love you, too. I can't wait for them to meet you, whether it's here or over there."

"I know I'll love them, too. They must be wonderful since they raised two great guys. I have a lot to thank them for." Her eyes misted. "Just know that I support you, Aleck, no matter what."

"Thanks, lass."

"So do I, big brother." Rory gave him a shoulder squeeze that turned into a back-slapping hug. "See you in the mornin'."

Aleck watched them go.

I guess you'd have to quit. That was exactly what Rory would do in his shoes. What he had done, in a sense, when he'd relocated to be close to Damaris. Aleck loved his brother with a fierce loyalty that would never change, but he was nothing like him. He didn't make rash decisions in the heat of the moment.

When he finally chose his path, whatever it was, it would be with the knowledge he'd looked at the issue from all angles, considered all the implications and made the best decision under the circumstances.

He turned to check on Tansy, who'd come out from behind the bar and was gazing in his direction. She beckoned to him. As he walked toward her, he admired the sassy tilt of her hat and her confident smile. God, how he loved that lass.

Her brown eyes were shining with excitement. "Michael said I could leave. He'll finish up."

"Great news."

"Did you want the rest of your beer? You left some over there."

"What do you think?"

She smiled. "Just wanted to ask. You paid for it."

"I got my money's worth, just knowin' I was in the same room with you."

"How about we trade this big room for something smaller?"

"You read my mind." He followed her over to the stairs at the back of the room and waited while she unhooked the velvet rope. He replaced it before starting up the stairs. "What's this I hear about a bear costume?"

"Rory must have told you."

"Aye. Didn't even know the GG would have a parade entry, let alone a dancin' bear."

"From what I hear, the GG has always been in the parade, but Bryce initiated the float concept when he bought the place. Before that I don't think anyone had floats. Now several businesses have them."

"I'm not sure what I pictured happenin' tomorrow, but likely it was more along the lines of kids with wagons, maybe a few antique cars, some horseback riders and maybe the high school band."

"Bryce showed me some old pictures and it used to be exactly like that. It's grown." She reached the top of the stairs. "Now we have an international entry."

"You do?"

She glanced over her shoulder. "That would be you, hotshot. And for the rest of the night, I'll have you all to myself."

He took the last few steps two at a time. Friday would be here before he knew it.

<u>26</u>

"Wait a minute." Tansy turned toward the doorway. "Can you stay outside for a little bit?" She pushed the door almost closed. "I need to do something."

"Change into your bear costume?"

"Would that turn you on?" She grabbed a box of kitchen matches and went around the room lighting the votive candles she'd bought at Pills and Pop on her way home from the ranch.

"I'd like to say it would, that anythin' you wear would get me hot, but I don't know about a bear costume."

"It's soft and furry." She finished lighting the candles and switched off the overhead and the lamp on her dresser. Then she folded back the covers on the bed. "You might have some fun with the texture."

"I like your regular texture. Smooth and silky does it for me."

"Then maybe I'll scrap the idea of the bear costume." She quickly stripped off her clothes. Boots were a pain when it came to undressing.

"I'd like you to model it later, though."

"Maybe when you model your plaid?"

"You want me to?"

"Well, duh. It's not every day I have a Highlander in my apartment, let alone one who brought his outfit."

"Then I'll be glad to put it on for you."

"Good, that's settled. Listen, would you take off your boots before you come in?"

"They're not muddy. I cleaned them before I...oh. Sure, I'd be glad to. How about my hat?"

"That's not as critical, but sure." She pulled her transparent cover-up over her head.

"Anythin' else you want me to take off?"

"Not while you're out on the landing. Most folks don't wander back this way, but we still have customers out there."

"Aye, right."

"Anyway, I'll have fun undressing you. Come on in."

He opened the door and walked in carrying his boots and hat. "Ah, lass." After he nudged the door closed, his gaze swept the candlelit apartment. "You did all this for me?"

He was so adorable. "Heavens, no. Lighting candles on Independence Day Eve is my personal tradition and you just happen to be here."

"Really?"

"I'm teasing. *Of course* I did it for you! I wanted tonight to be special."

He set down his boots and balanced his hat on top of them. "It was always goin' to be special." Eliminating the distance between them, he drew her close. "But knowin' that you spent time to create this settin' humbles me. I wish I'd brought you flowers."

"That's a lovely thought, but it would have been tricky." She wound her arms around his neck. "You came in with a crowd and had to sneak up to my apartment to leave your duffle. There's no room in that scenario for bringing me flowers."

"Were the candles here when I came up before?"

"Yes, but I'm sure you were too distracted to notice."

"Guess so." His green eyes held the soft glow she'd come to cherish. "I'm just sayin' that I would have loved to bring you flowers."

"You brought me you. That's all I need." She rose on tiptoe and brushed a kiss over his lips. "Will you let me undress you? That would be way more exciting to me than a bouquet."

He smiled. "Like you said, you've seen it all before."

"Not recently." She eased away and slid her hands under the hem of his shirt. "And never in candlelight."

He touched her hair. "I love the way it gleams in your hair."

"Highlighting all those crazy colors?" She pushed the T-shirt higher to reveal the shadowed magnificence of his chest.

"I like the colors." He combed his fingers through her hair and tucked it behind her ears. "Makes me smile."

"Your manly chest makes *me* smile. Lift your arms so I can get this off."

He chuckled. "Gettin' a wee bit bossy, are we?"

"Your T-shirt is more of an obstacle than I thought." She tugged it over his head and peeled it away from his muscled arms.

"Whereas this flimsy thing is no obstacle at all." He stroked his knuckles over the tip of her breast. "There's a flower printed right here. I'm thinkin' that's no accident." He lazily brushed back and forth.

Logically the subtle caress shouldn't be enough to make her core muscles clench. She gasped as a tremor rolled through her. She caught his hand.

"Am I botherin' you, lass?"

Heart racing, she lifted her gaze to his. "Yes."

"Want to do somethin' about it?"

She swallowed. "I haven't finished undressing you."

"I can have these jeans off and a condom on in under thirty seconds. Does that interest you at all?"

"Yes, damn it." She stepped back and pulled off her cover-up. "I think it's the candles." She glanced around at all those tiny flames, which seemed to have ignited an out-of-control blaze in her. "I thought they were supposed to make everything mellow and romantic."

"Instead they turned you into a lusty wench." He'd made good on his boast. He was already naked with a condom in his hand.

"Evidently." She focused on his erect tadger. "All I can think about is—"

"Then we're thinkin' alike." He rolled on the condom. "But since you've a mind to be in charge tonight, let's do it this way." He stretched out on her bed. "Climb aboard."

"Heck, yeah." She crawled onto the bed. "I'm about to make you my own personal playground."

He laughed. "If this is you on candlelight, I want more of it."

"I guess it is." She surveyed the tempting expanse of male beauty stretched out on her bed. The flickering glow made him seem even more god-like than he had the day before. "I've never gone total candlelight before. I'm a fan. You look delicious."

"So do you, lass. I hope you'll start doin' somethin' soon, or I'm liable to take back the reins."

"Listen to you! Riding for two days and you're talking like a horseman."

"I have a different kind of ridin' in mind. Come closer."

"I will, but hands off. Remember yesterday?"

"Vividly."

"We're going to recreate your opening move with me in the lead position. Lie back and let me explore."

He sucked in a breath. "Not sure I can handle that without explodin'."

"Do your best." Leaning over him, she placed a restraining hand on each of his forearms as she nibbled on his mouth. "I want you to just lie there and take it like a man."

He groaned in protest, but he didn't try to escape, even though he could have brushed aside her puny attempts with no effort at all. Made bold by the power he'd given her, she began her sensuous trek over his body, taking her cues from his methods from the day before.

The outer shell of his ear was sensitive, but not the hollow of his throat. He twitched when she licked her way along his collarbone and down the muscled curve of his bicep. He moaned when she sucked on his fingers.

But she didn't get an off-the-chart reaction until she made love to his pecs and toyed with his nipples. His breathing grew harsh and his tadger jerked.

"Lass..." His gaze turned stormy and he gulped for air. "For the love of God...please...I need...

"Okay." She'd meant to give him the full body treatment, but he was clearly in distress. Truth be told, so was she. His response had stoked the fire in her until she was trembling.

Sliding one leg over his torso, she rose on hands and knees. "One stupendous orgasm, coming up." She grasped his tadger at the base, centered herself and took him in one smooth motion.

Panting, he caught her hips and held her tight. "Don't move."

She gulped. "Like I could. You've got me pinned."

"Am I...hurting you?" He squeezed his eyes shut.

"No. I'm just...immobilized."

"I don't want to come yet." He clenched his jaw. "This is too good."

"Take your time." She sucked in another breath. "We have all night."

"And we'll do this...some more."

"Planned on it."

He slowly opened his eyes. "I'm going to let go. Take it easy."

She smiled. "Be gentle?"

"Gentle but firm." He swallowed. "Just like—"

"Brushing a horse." She moved slowly, tenderly, gauging his response, keeping her climax in check, telling him with her body what she hadn't said with her words.

He licked his lips. "More."

"Faster?"

"Aye."

She eased off the brakes and allowed herself the increased friction she craved. "How's that?"

"Good. More."

"Alrighty. Full speed ahead."

He flashed her a grin. "Go for it, Tansy-girl."

Did she ever. She gave it all she had, and his brogue thickened as he alternately gasped and swore...and came with one vigorous thrust.

That was all she needed to draw her into the whirling vortex with him. She would have yelled if she'd had the breath to do it. Shuddering, she slowly sank down and rested her forehead against his. "I'm wrung out."

His chest heaved. "Aye. Me, too." He rubbed her back, caressing her with slow, lazy strokes. "In a good way."

"So good." Lifting her head, she gazed into his beautiful eyes. "I'm in the mood for a cuddle. How about you?"

"I'm always in the mood for a cuddle with you, lass. Let me up and we'll get situated."

She slowly ended their sweet connection and got out of bed. "I'm setting my phone alarm. We can't afford to oversleep in the morning."

"Mine's already set for five so I can try Campbell again." He ducked into the bathroom.

"Oh, right. I'll set mine, anyway. Might as well have two alerts." She crawled back into bed and tidied the covers. "After we cuddle for a bit, will you model your tartan for me?"

"Aye." He came out of the bathroom. "The tartan in exchange for the bear suit."

"It's a deal."

He climbed in and drew her close. "Glad you suggested this. Cozy."

"I know." Snuggling against him, she laid her cheek against his chest and sighed. "We could have a blether."

He chuckled and kissed the top of her head. "Aye, we could, at that. What's the scent in your shampoo?"

"Do you like it?"

"I do."

"It's called Ambrosia. Has a combination of things in it."

"No wonder I couldn't pick out any particular one. Suits you."

"Thanks. A local woman makes it."

"So you can't get it anywhere, then?"

"Just at Pills and Pop for now. She's thinking of expanding her distribution, but for now it's an Eagles Nest exclusive." She shifted positions and gazed up at him. "And since we're blethering, I'd love to hear more about your apple-shoveling experience."

He tensed.

"Or not." She gulped as the glow in his eyes faded. "You said we'd talk about it later, but if you've changed your mind, that's okay. It's really none of my business."

"It is your business, lass." Sadness filled his gaze. "I thought I'd come up with a bonnie answer for us. But it wouldn't work, after all."

Her breath caught. "You were trying to figure out how we could be together?"

"Aye. I suppose you have been doin' that, too, but there's—"

"No, I haven't." Her chest grew tight.

"You haven't? Why not? I know you care for me. I see it in your eyes."

"Aleck, I come from a family of lawyers. I know first-hand how hard they worked to get where they are. Rory had a difficult decision to make but you'd have an impossible one."

"That's why I was goin' to ask you to move to Scotland."

She swallowed. "I wouldn't go. No matter how much I...care for you, it would be a huge mistake."

"This mornin' I couldn't see that. Now I can." He drew in a shaky breath. "What are we to do, then?"

She cupped his face in both hands. His beard was silky against her palms. "You're going to model your tartan for me and I'm going to put on my bear suit. And we'll make love again, because finding something this wonderful is a gift."

"Aye." His voice was husky. "So 'tis, lass."

27

While Tansy pulled her bear suit out of a drawer, Aleck unpacked his tartan. They'd agreed to dress with their backs to each other and turn around when they were done.

A zipper rasped as Tansy prepared to climb into her bear suit. "Does this remind you of anything?"

"Our adventures on the front porch of the ranch house?"

"Exactly."

"My tadger suffered that night."

"Speaking of which, are you wearing anything under your kilt?"

"Now or tomorrow?"

"Tomorrow. Damaris can't get Rory to tell her what he's doing."

"That's because he's wearin' briefs and he wants to keep the mystery alive. A true Scotsman doesn't wear anythin', but it could be breezy tomorrow. I'm wearin' 'em, too, and I'll not be discussin' it with anyone but you."

"My lips are sealed. But please don't feel you have to wear them now."

"I assumed that was the whole point." He tucked his white linen shirt into his kilt and buckled it.

"You assumed correctly."

He smiled. She wasn't going to let the dark cloud of impending separation ruin their special night together. Not his Tansy-girl.

He would follow her lead. "Can I skip the socks and brogues, too? And the tam?"

"Sure. I just want the main stuff. The sexy stuff."

After putting on his sporran, he unfolded his plaid and pinned it into place. "Then I'm done."

"Me, too." Her voice was muffled. "Don't look now, but there's a bear behind you."

He turned and choked on a laugh. The suit's eyeholes convinced him that Tansy was in there, but otherwise he never would have known. "That's...that's..."

"Hysterical?"

"Aye." He couldn't stop grinning. "What kind of bear is it supposed to be?"

"A grizzly, of course." She lifted her paws. "Grrr."

"You're too cute for words."

"And you're too sexy for words. Can I take this off so I can touch your gorgeous plaid?"

"Let me take it off. I've never undressed a bear before."

"Be my guest. It unzips down the back." She turned around. "The top of the zipper is at the back of the head."

"Found it. This material is soft and furry, just like you said."

"And hot. Oh, my God, I'm going to roast tomorrow."

He drew the zipper down, careful not to catch it in her hair.

She grasped the bear's snout and pulled the top of the suit off her head. "Whew. Good thing the parade is early in the morning when it's still cool."

"You could wear it naked." He leaned over to kiss his way down her bare back. "That would be cooler."

"I wish I had the nerve. Just my luck something would happen that would mean taking it off. Nope, not doing it. I have my limits, just like you with your briefs."

The zipper ended at the small of her back. He placed one last kiss there before standing so he could slide the costume off her arms. "Gettin' you out of this bear suit is more excitin' than I expected. It's like one of those stories where the animal turns into a lovely lass durin' a full moon."

"And the handsome prince has to find a way to break the spell so they can be together."

"Aye." He gave the suit a push and it fell to the floor in a furry heap. "Abracadabra, the spell is broken. You're free." If only all spells could be so easily broken.

"Thank you, kind prince." She stepped out of the costume, folded it and laid it on top of the dresser. "Or should I say clan chief?"

"Canna be, since my grandfather's still around." He reached for her.

She moved away. "Hands off, my brave Highlander. I'm still inspecting your outfit. Your grandfather's a clan chief?"

"Possibly. He's doin' research on it but the records are murky. We call him our clan chief because it makes us happy to do it, but we have no historical proof yet."

"That's very cool." She came closer and fingered the antique medallion pinned at his shoulder. "Just like Rory's."

"You've seen his?"

"He and Damaris showed me his plaid and the medallion, but he hasn't worn it for anyone but Damaris, yet." She smoothed her hand over the section of wool stretched across his chest. "I love the dark blue and green. Very manly."

"Just so you know, this manly man is havin' trouble keepin' his hands to himself with you standin' there naked and strokin' his chest."

"Just give me a little more time to admire you." Her gaze moved down. "A sporran, right?"

"Right."

"It just moved."

"I'm not surprised."

She stepped back. "You're magnificent, Aleck McGavin. I could eat you up."

"Right back at you, lass. Can I touch you, now?"

"Soon, after you take everything off. But I'd love to have just one kiss while you're wearing the tartan for my memory book in my head."

"A memory book in your head. That's brilliant."

"Thank you." Candlelight flickered in her eyes. "I don't want to rumple anything. Can we do that without going into overload?"

"I can."

"So can I." In three steps, she was in his arms. "The wool is so soft."

"Not as soft as you." He held her gently, tamping down his response as he dipped his head, closed his eyes and lightly pressed his mouth against hers. *Ta gra agam duit.* Then he let her go.

She backed away, stars in her eyes. "That was so lovely."

His throat tightened. "Aye."

"How about if I sit on the bed and watch you take everything off?"

"How about if you search my jeans pocket first?"

She smiled. "I could do that."

When she had the condom in her hand, he unpinned the medallion and tucked it back in its place in his duffle. Much as he wanted her, he couldn't rush this.

"How long have you had that outfit?"

"My grandpa gave it to me on my twenty-first birthday. It's supposed to last me a long time." He folded the plaid carefully and laid it in next to the medallion.

"What if you put on weight?"

"I have."

"Where? I didn't notice an ounce of flab on you."

"I've added some muscle since then." He pulled the linen shirt over his head.

"Exhibit A. But the shirt still fits."

"It's a generous cut." He put it on top of the plaid. "The shirt's the easiest thing to replace, though. If I spill on it or rip it somehow, I can get a new one, no problem. Not so much with the plaid and the kilt. That's why I'll change right after the parade. Rory's bringing clothes for both of us. We're not spendin' the day in our tartans." He laid his sporran on top of the rest.

She sighed. "Wish I could see you two do your thing."

"Kendra said the local photographer—what's her name?"

"Caitlin Dempsey."

"Right. She'll be taking video of the parade and it'll be posted on the town website." He unbuckled his kilt.

"How does it feel?"

"Pardon?"

"Wearing the kilt with nothing underneath."

"Turns me into a randy Scotsman."

"Does it really?"

"See for yourself." He stepped out of the kilt.

She sucked in a breath.

"Appreciate the gasp, Tansy-girl, but why? As we've established, you've seen it all before."

"I know, but taking off a kilt is a thousand times sexier than pulling off jeans and briefs."

"It is?"

"Nobody's told you?"

"Nobody's seen me do it before."

"Really? This is a first?"

"One of many." He folded the kilt and put it away before crossing to the bed. He held out his hand. "May I have that wee packet?"

She gave it to him. "I didn't realize what I was asking. Do you ever wear it with nothing underneath?"

"No."

"So that part about turning into a randy Scotsman was—"

"Teasin' you, lass." He rolled on the condom. "This has nothin' to do with my kilt and everythin' to do with you. Scoot over. I'm comin' in."

She made room for him and he wasted no time sliding between her silken thighs. Braced on his forearms, he leaned down and kissed her deeply and thoroughly before easing his aching tadger into her heat.

Lifting his head, he held her gaze as he began to stroke.

She hugged him close, rising to meet each thrust. When she wrapped her legs around his, tightening their connection, his boundaries blurred. They moved as one.

No words. His body spoke to hers in a language that transcended time and space. No urgency. Only this steady, mesmerizing rhythm. She opened like a flower to the sun, claiming her release as easily as breathing. He followed in a shimmering cascade of wonder.

Perfect.

28

So much love. Tansy's heart overflowed with it. Aleck didn't speak as he quietly left the bed. When he came out of the bathroom, he made a circuit of the apartment to blow out all the candles. Then he slipped in beside her and gathered her close. Cradled in his arms, she was asleep in seconds.

She woke to the sound of his voice. The milky light of dawn filtered in through the street-side window, outlining Aleck sitting at her dinette table, his phone to his ear.

He spoke in a low voice. "I know it is. Aye. See you on Saturday."

The conversation ended. He laid the phone on the table and put his head in his hands.

"Aleck?"

Startled, he left the chair and came toward her. "Damn, I'm sorry. I was trying to be quiet so I wouldn't wake you."

"It's okay. I should get up soon, anyway." She climbed out of bed and met him halfway. He'd put on his jeans, as if he hadn't wanted to call his boss while naked. "You don't look happy."

"I forgot about the bloody fundraiser in September. The firm's a major sponsor. Campbell's paid for a table and we're all expected to be there."

"Could you reimburse him?"

"He doesn't want the money back. He wants me sitting at that table."

"People have conflicts. You can't be the only—"

"For this event, nothing short of getting hit by a bus cuts it."

"Really?"

"It's his favorite charity and he expects us to bid generously during the auction. Historically our firm raises the most." He ran his fingers through his hair. "I should have remembered the date, but I—"

"You had other things on your mind."

"Aye." He reached for her and gathered her close. "I'm so sorry, lass."

She hugged him tight and put a smile on her face. "No apology necessary. I grew up with this. You've carved out a place for yourself and you have to be a team player to keep it."

"I hate to disappoint Badger."

"He's not your responsibility. He's resourceful. He'll figure it out."

The frown line was back. "I guess I was countin' on September more than I thought."

She had been, too, judging from the way her chest ached. But no point in making the situation worse by saying so. "Hey, you'll be back soon, maybe even with your folks."

"Rory wants all three of us to come over for Christmas."

"That would be terrific." Six months. An eternity.

"Now that September's fallen through, I could probably swing the time off." He paused. "Except Campbell always schedules the firm's Christmas party close to the twenty-fifth because he says its more festive."

"Another command performance?"

"Definitely. I've heard people complain that it made their travel plans a challenge but I never used to care. Didn't affect me."

"Your boss sounds like a man of strong opinions." And not much regard for the wishes of others.

"Aye, he is that." He gazed down at her. "I hate this."

She massaged his tense shoulders. "We still have today."

"Hope you won't mind if I stick to you like glue."

"Fine with me. Speaking of that, we can buddy up for the three-legged race if you want."

"Absolutely. I asked Rory to bring my trainers. When do you have to start work?"

"I offered to help Michael set up at three, but I won't officially bartend until six. I'll be off at eleven, though, if you want to stay here again tonight."

He sighed. "Wish I could, lass. Meant to say somethin' about that and didn't." He tucked her in closer. "My flight's early—only one I could get when I had to change my reservation."

"How early?"

"Rory will be takin' me around four in the mornin'."

"Ouch."

"Worse yet, now I'll have my pipes to worry about so we might decide to go earlier." His frown deepened. "I'd give anything to spend those last hours with you, but all things considered, I—"

"It would be a huge hassle. That's okay."

"No, it's not okay." He cupped her face in both hands. "It's well shan, is what it is, and yet there you are, smilin' at me."

"Because you're pure barry." She gazed into his beloved face. "The pure barriest."

"Ah, lass." He lowered his head and brushed her lips with his. "My Tansy-girl." His kiss was gentle at first, but began to heat up.

So did she...until her phone's chime doused the flame. The cheerful tune had appealed to her once. She'd change it out for something else today.

He drew back. "We can't be late. I promised Rory I'd be down there when he pulls in."

"Then you take the first shower. I don't have to walk down there with—"

"Oh, yes, you do, lass. I've got one more day and I'm not lettin' you out of my sight. You take first shower. I can get ready in no time now that I don't have to shave."

She stroked his beard. "Will you keep this when you go home?"

The sparkle left his eyes.

"You'll have to shave it?"

"Aye."

"Damn. I love that beard on you." *I love you.* She turned and walked into the bathroom before she said it out loud. Now was not the time. The way things were going, that time might never come.

* * *

Aleck stuck to his plan of spending every available minute of the day with Tansy. After six, that meant hanging out in the Guzzling Grizzly tent where she was serving drinks. He pitched in to deliver them during the crazy-busy dinner hour and he had to turn down several tips.

Since his friends and family knew where to find him, he had plenty of visitors, including Badger, who was disappointed but understanding about the wedding. Hugs and handshakes were in plentiful supply from McGavins, Sawyers and Bennetts. Tansy claimed he was good for business. Nearly everyone who came to say goodbye also bought a drink.

A little before ten, Rory showed up, his expression sad but resigned. "Hate to nudge you, big brother, but if we're gettin' up in a few hours, we'd better—"

"I keep hopin' Caitlin will arrive with the video." A large screen, a projector, a folding table and an extension cord were sitting in the back of Ryker's truck in case she made it before the event ended.

But she'd warned them not to expect miracles. She'd finished videoing only a few hours ago. She was too much of a pro to slap something together.

"She's here!" Damaris rushed over and nearly lost her glasses in her excitement. "They're setting everything up!"

"Excellent." Aleck headed toward the makeshift bar where Tansy and Michael were working side-by-side filling drink orders. "She's here."

Tansy looked up, her gaze triumphant. "Told you."

"That's awesome." Michael reached behind him. "We're not missing this." He taped a hand-lettered *On Break* sign to the bar. "Let's go to the movies."

"I'm right behind you." She joined Aleck, Rory and Damaris while Michael went in search of Roxanne. "See? I knew Caitlin would get it done. Now we can all watch it together."

"That we can, lass." He slipped an arm around her waist as they walked toward an open area in front of the bandstand. A crowd was already gathering.

Ryker and Badger were setting up a large screen and anchoring it to the floor while Aaron unloaded the folding table. Then he unwound the extension cord while Caitlin plugged in the projector.

Aunt Kendra came over and gave him a friendly jab with her elbow. "See? I knew she'd get it done in time for you to see it."

He laughed. "You and Tansy must be reading from the same script. She said the same thing."

"Because she knows how things work around here. The good guys always win. Or in this case, the good gal. I'll bet she's exhausted, but she did it. She's the best."

"I know she's good. Her pictures from Ryker and April's weddin' were outstandin'. I'm especially interested in what she got of the parade."

"That's what I'm after." Quinn walked over and put his arm around Kendra's shoulder. "I tried my damnedest to switch with that guy driving the tricked-out hearse so I'd be behind Raptors Rise. He has suspension lifts on that blasted vehicle and my Harley sits low. I couldn't see the dance."

"Poor baby." Kendra patted his cheek. "We'll make sure Ellie Mae does a better job of assigning numbers next year."

Rory chuckled. "Ellie Mae was flirtin' with Aleck like you wouldn't believe. Kept askin' if he was okay with our position behind the precision drill team. She didn't want him steppin' in horse apples in his brogues."

"Well, damn," Quinn said. "When *I* asked her about switching, she just smiled and said the other guy liked his spot and I'd need to work it out with him. Next year I'm wearing a kilt."

"Oh, *yeah*." Kendra fanned herself. "Another fantasy fulfilled. If you'd learn to play the pipes, I—"

"Hi, everybody!" Caitlin's braids were coming unraveled and her shirt looked as if she'd spilled a drink on it, but her expression was incandescent. "We're ready to roll the video. Hope you like it!"

"Let's hear it for Caitlin!" Aaron started the round of applause that included cheers and whistles. A crowd of high school kids shouted *We love you, Caitlin!*

She blushed and took a bow before turning to the laptop and starting the video.

After an intro identifying the event, Ryker, Badger and Aaron rode toward the camera wearing identical military uniforms and grasping rippling flags of the U.S., Montana and Eagles Nest. Ryker, a guy clearly made to lead a parade, occupied the center position on Jake.

The high school band came next, followed by a float for Crimson Clouds, the guest ranch run by Quinn's eldest son Pete and his sweetheart Taryn Maroney. They threw out wrapped candy to the kids in the crowd. The town council smiled and waved from the back of an antique fire truck.

An excellent sound system on the GG float projected Bryce and Nicole's version of *Born in the USA* as several more antique vehicles rolled by. Then the float appeared.

"One dancing bear, coming up," Tansy murmured.

"Can't wait." He leaned down and gave her a quick kiss. When his attention returned to the screen, his heart squeezed. She'd told him that she'd nearly melted in that costume, yet she was dancing her heart out, wiggling her cute little bum and adding all sorts of fancy arm movements.

"I look demented."

"You look pure barry. The pure barriest." He tightened his grip. He'd be watching that section over and over once he got home. Thank the Lord for the Internet.

The precision drill team came next, and then he and Rory filled the screen performing *Scotland the Brave*.

Ma and Da would love seeing this. He glanced at Rory and smiled. His brother grinned and gave a nod.

Tansy sucked in a breath. "You're beautiful."

"Men aren't beautiful, lass."

"You are." She gulped. Then she sniffed.

He glanced down and she was using her free hand to thumb tears from her eyes. He gently turned her toward him and she buried her face against his chest. When her hat threatened to fall off, he lifted it free and used it to shield her emotional reaction from view.

Rory looked over and raised his eyebrows.

"Meet you by the truck as soon as it's over."

"Aye."

Aleck kept a protective arm around Tansy's shoulders as they made their way through the crowd. Luckily the park was at the same end of town as the GG, so they didn't have far to go before they were standing by Rory's truck. The lot was filled with the overflow from the park.

Releasing her, he pulled his bandana out of his back pocket. "Here."

"Th-thanks." She wiped her eyes and blew her nose. Then she gazed at him and had to do it all over again. "I was doing fine, until..."

"You're still doin' fine."

"No, I'm not. I want you to carry home a memory of me smiling and happy, not red-eyed and sniffling."

"I'll carry home a memory of every second I've been lucky enough to be near you. It's been such a privilege, lass."

She stared at him as new tears streamed down her face. "For...for me, too."

"Come here, Tansy-girl." Drawing her into his arms, he held her close, rubbing her back with his free hand and making sure he didn't drop her hat. Or start bawling himself.

They stayed like that until Rory and Damaris arrived.

Taking a shaky breath, she eased out of his arms and wiped her eyes again before she faced them. "Sorry about the waterworks."

"Been there," Damaris said softly. "Come on." She motioned to her. "I'll walk you back to the park. We'll take our time so you can get it together."

"But aren't you going home with the guys?"

"No room."

"I forgot about that, Damaris," Aleck said. "I'll ride in back."

"We've already worked it out. Kendra's giving me a ride in the van." She glanced at Tansy. "But I can also come back with you and stay the night if you'd rather not be alone."

"That's so nice of you, but...I'll be fine." She turned to Aleck. "I'll be fine."

He ached all over. "I know you will."

"Bye, Aleck."

"Bye, Tansy-girl."

"Let's go, big brother." Rory's voice was gruff with distress.

"Aye." He climbed in the truck, closed the door and avoided looking in the side-view mirror. He might see her walking away. "I've never felt this bad in my whole miserable life."

Rory nodded and started the engine. "Like Damaris said, been there."

29

They drove back to the ranch in silence.

When Rory pulled up in front of the ranch house, Aleck turned to him. "There's no way I'm goin' to sleep."

"I know. You just need to get the hell out of here."

"Right."

He shut off the engine. "Tell you what. I'll go in with you while you finish packin' up. Then I'll take you to Bozeman. There's a bar that might be open since it's the Fourth. If not, we'll sit in the airport until time for you to check in."

"You don't have to do that. I can—"

"I'm not leavin' you."

"Thanks, Rory."

"Hey, what are brothers for?"

He gave him a weak smile. "Bailin' each other out of guddles?"

"That's the way I've always looked at it. Let's do this."

"Aye." As he walked beside his brother up the path, his boots clicked on the flagstone. "You were right about the gravitas."

"You wearin' the hat and boots on the plane, then?"

"I am."

"Good."

"I just remembered. I was goin' to take beer home to Ma and Da."

"Don't worry about it. Wouldn't stay temperature controlled anyway. Better if they drink it for the first time whenever they get here."

"I'll try for Christmas."

"That would make a lot of people very happy. One in particular."

"Uh-huh." He walked into the house and handed Rory his hat. "I'll be back in no time."

"I'll brush the lint off it for you. Doesn't look quite as pristine as it used to."

"Don't brush anythin' off. If there's a couple of Tansy's hairs on there, that's just fine with me."

Rory opened his mouth to say something.

"Don't even start. I know I'm a bampot." He hurried down the hall to get his things together and was done in under five minutes. Out of habit, he checked his passport holder before tucking it in an outside pocket of his carry-on.

It was empty.

Swearing under his breath, he went through his suitcase. What the hell? Searched his carry-on. Looked all over the room, under the bed, behind the dresser.

"Aleck? You movin' furniture in there?"

"Can't find my damned passport."

"What?" Rory's quick footsteps ended when he appeared in the doorway. "How could you lose it?"

"Hell if I know, but I've searched through everything."

"Did you make a copy and tuck it in your suitcase? That'll work."

"I didn't make one."

"Why not? You always tell me—"

"I know what I always tell you. But when I renewed I never got around to doin' that."

"Could you have somehow left it at Tansy's?"

"I don't see how, but I'd better ask." He picked up his phone and sent her a text.

She replied quickly. *I'm almost done here. I'll go home and look.*

He glanced up. "She'll look."

"Might as well go through your stuff one more time."

He sighed. "Might as well." He checked more thoroughly, sliding his hand into pockets and unfolding clothes. "It's not here."

"Could it be in my truck?"

"That's an idea. I'll comb through the house while you scour the truck."

Rory came back empty-handed. "Nothin'?"

"Nothin'. I've pulled up couch cushions, crawled around so I can see under the furniture, checked the kitchen, even looked behind the washer and dryer in the laundry room." He stared at his brother. "I can't believe this."

"I can't either. You're the most careful and organized person I know."

"Maybe somehow it ended up at Tansy's. Ah, there's her text." He read it. "Not there."

"Now what?"

"I'm not goin' anywhere, that's what. I had a client who had this happen. It's not an easy fix. They were stuck in Spain for a week or more."

"That's not good. I'm sorry, big brother. Damn, where do you suppose it could be?" He surveyed the living room as if hoping it lay in plain sight.

"I don't know." He couldn't get on a plane unless it turned up and that didn't seem likely after they'd searched everywhere.

If he didn't make that flight, he'd miss the meeting. Campbell wouldn't believe his story. Losing a passport was not like him, not like him at all. Campbell would accuse him of lying about it.

He waited for panic to start gnawing at his gut. He could lose his job over this. Lose everything he'd worked for. He should be sweating bullets and frantically trying to figure out a way to save the situation.

But he wasn't. Instead a soothing calm spread from the top of his head to the tip of his toes. He took a deep breath and exhaled. Happiness followed on the heels of that cleansing flow of peaceful energy.

He smiled.

"Aleck?"

"What?"

"Did you just figure out where it is?"

"No." He gazed at Rory. "I don't know where it is. And I don't care."

His brother's eyes widened. "Who are you and what have you done with my brother?"

"I'm quitting, Rory. I'm not going to think about it for months or study the pros and cons until I'm blue in the face. I love Tansy with everything in me and she loves me back just as much. Why in hell wouldn't I move here?"

"Because you can't work as a lawyer over here? Because that's all you know how to do and you'd have to go back to school to get certified?"

"You've been doing your research."

"I looked it up because I needed to know. How will you make a living?"

"I don't know, but I'm not worried about it. I'll figure it out. I'll go back to school if I decide to. I'll wait tables at the GG to bring in cash."

"Muck out stables?"

"Hell, yeah. I'll shovel horse apples for Aunt Kendra if she needs another hand. I'll do whatever it takes." He took a breath. "Would you be willin' to drive me back to the GG?"

A happy grin spread across his brother's face. "Aye."

* * *

Rory's bringing me in. Please unlock the back door of the GG.

Tansy read the text several times before replying. Evidently Aleck thought he could find that passport even though she'd turned her apartment upside down looking for it. He was welcome to try. She hoped he was successful, poor guy.

She texted a reply. *When you guys get here, we'll transfer your stuff to my truck so Rory can go home. If you find it, I'll drive you to Bozeman.*

His reply had been cryptic. *We can talk about that when I get there.*

Talk about what? Nothing to talk about. Losing his passport must be driving him nuts. It was so out of character. She hated this for him.

If he couldn't find it, he'd be stranded in Eagles Nest until he got a new one. She was fuzzy on the details of how that worked, but it couldn't be easy.

He wouldn't be a happy camper while navigating whatever red tape was involved. Clearly his boss was an inflexible autocrat who would interpret this mishap as a personal insult to his authority. Aleck could get sacked. Made her stomach hurt.

Pocketing her truck keys, she went downstairs and out the back to wait. She didn't often lock her truck, but if they were putting his luggage and pipes in there, she would.

She paced in the area illuminated by the security light over the door. Aleck wasn't the only one stressed. When he and Rory had driven away tonight, unbearable pain had sliced through her. For a little while, she wondered if it would ever get better. But with Damaris's gentle support, she'd managed to make it through the last of her shift.

By the time Kendra and Damaris had walked her back home when the event was over, she'd begun the difficult process of letting go. Now she'd have to go through it all over again. She wasn't looking forward to that.

Aleck was in the same fix, except he had the added weight of a career in jeopardy. Damn it, why did he have to go and lose his passport?

The rumble of a truck's engine kicked her heartbeat into high gear. Rory came down the alley using only his parking lights and backed into his usual spot. Aleck climbed out.

Even the dire circumstances couldn't dampen her joy at seeing him again. "I'm so sorry." She walked toward him and pulled out her keys. "Let's get your things moved. I'll lock my truck so there's no chance that—"

"Didn't bring my stuff." He turned to shut the door. "Thanks, Rory. See you tomorrow."

"You bet." When the door was closed, he pulled out.

"You didn't bring your luggage? What if you find your passport in my apartment?"

"I've stopped lookin' for it." Nudging back his hat, he walked toward her.

His brave smile made her chest ache. "You don't have to pretend to be okay with this. I know how this could affect your future and I—"

"I'm not sure you do." His smile didn't dim. If anything, it grew brighter.

"Well, maybe not fully, but your boss doesn't seem like the sort to let this pass."

"Oh, he's not." He drew her into his arms. "And I don't give a damn."

"What?"

"He's through messin' with me, lass."

"You're going to stand up to him?"

"In a manner of speakin'. When I get back, whenever that is, I'm handin' in my resignation."

"Hang on, Aleck. Don't go throwing the baby out with the bathwater. What if he's just a bully who'll back down?"

"I don't care if he does or not. I don't want that job anymore."

"Oh." She paused. "That's valid. And if you quit instead of getting fired, you'll be in a good position to find something better." She smiled. "That's how a Highlander would think."

"I've already found somethin' better."

"Wow, that was quick. Are law offices already open in Scotland?"

"Some might be, but I haven't called anybody there." He reached for her. "I've found somethin' better right here."

She stared at him. "I don't get it."

His gaze gentled. "I love you, Tansy-girl. It's as simple as that."

The breath whooshed out of her lungs. He couldn't possibly mean...

"I'm leavin' Scotland."

She gulped and shook her head. "No. You can't just—"

"Ah, but I can." He cupped her face and brushed his thumbs over her cheekbones. "I couldn't see it until I lost my passport. To my surprise, instead of worryin' myself sick about the consequences, I started thinkin' about the possibilities." His gaze held hers. "They all start with you, lass."

Tears pushed at the back of her eyes. She would start blubbering any second. "But you'd...you'd give up so much."

"And get so much in return. Everythin' I thought was so important was only weighin' me down."

She swallowed. "This is such a huge decision. I hope...I hope you know what you're doing."

"I know what I'm doin'. I'm standin' beside a dumpster in the exact spot where I first discovered I loved you. And where I saw in your eyes you loved me back. I'm askin' you to take me into your heart for good, lass."

Tears dribbled down her cheeks. "You're already there, Aleck McGavin." She took a shaky breath. "*Ta gra agam duit.*"

His face lit up. "You learned it!"

His pleased astonishment was worth all the effort she'd made. "I didn't know if I'd ever get to say it. I love you so much. I couldn't help loving you, even when I didn't think we'd ever—"

"Break the spell?" Leaning forward, he kissed away the tears. "It's well and truly broken, lass. And you know how the story ends."

"Don't you mean how the story begins?"

"Aye." He smiled. "How it begins." His mouth found hers.

Epilogue

Flying for Badger Air had to be the best damn job in the world. Aaron couldn't imagine anything better than working as a civilian pilot with two of his buddies from the squadron, and this day had been exceptionally awesome. Co-piloting for Badger while he tested a Cessna 206 Stationair that would likely become the third commuter plane in their fleet had been a hoot.

"Can't believe I'll be Mr. Hayley Bennett soon." Badger banked the Cessna to the right, giving Aaron a view of Eagles Nest.

"You're gonna be *who*?"

"I asked her if she'd be changin' her name when we get married. She's agreed to be Mrs. Badger Calhoun if I'll be Mr. Hayley Bennett."

Aaron snorted.

"You laugh, but I think it's a stupendous idea and I'm holdin' her to it. I can't wait to start usin' my new name. I'll never have to be Thaddeus Livingston Calhoun the Third again."

"Is that legal?"

"Can't see why not. I'm orderin' personalized stationery so I'll have it on hand when the big day comes. I plan to write my thank-you notes on it."

"Only you, Badger."

"You think I'm kiddin' but I'm not. By the way, how do you like the monkey suits we picked out for the groomsmen? You okay with the style?"

"It's great. I look so handsome in that outfit I might actually make a favorable impression on someone of the opposite sex."

"Come to think of it, I haven't been hearin' a whole lot about your social life lately. Goin' through a dry spell?"

"You could say that."

"You doin' anythin' about it?"

"Like what?"

"Like askin' someone out."

"That's the thing. The person I'd like to ask out isn't a possibility."

"So try somebody else."

"Don't want to. I'm stuck on her and I can't seem to work up any enthusiasm for another woman."

"Sounds serious. Is she with someone? Is that the issue?"

"She's available."

"And she turned you down?"

"I didn't bother to ask. It's hopeless."

"Hopeless? You're decent lookin', you don't smell bad and you're a jet jockey. Ladies go for pilots."

"She has a problem with my name."

"Raven?"

"I doubt she knows what you guys call me. It's my legal one she doesn't like."

"How could she have a problem with your name? If you had one like mine, then, yeah. But yours is fine."

"She had a relationship with somebody named Aaron Donahue and it went very bad. She claims she could never get past my name."

"Huh. What are the chances?"

"Pretty good, apparently. Aaron Donahue is one of the more common names in this country. I looked it up."

"You really like her?"

"Yeah, I really do."

"Then we need to get her to fall for somebody with a different name who turns out to be you."

"How in the hell could you do that?"

"I'm not sure yet, but lucky for you this kind of thing is in my wheelhouse. Let me work out some details and get back to you. Who is it, by the way?"

"Caitlin Dempsey."

"Ah, good choice. This'll be fun."

Former Air Force pilot Aaron Donahue needs a new approach and a new name to win over Caitlin Dempsey in A COWBOY'S SECRET, book sixteen in the McGavin Brothers series!

* * * * *

Aaron polished off his beer before glancing over the latest version of his letter to Caitlin. "I think it's okay, but I can't tell anymore. My brain cells are still fried from your bachelor party." He handed it to Badger. "Take a look."

Badger scanned the paper and slid it back across the kitchen table. "You nailed it. Just needs a closin' and a signature."

"What kind of closing?"

Tilting back his chair and steepling his fingers, Badger maintained his balance with the same coordination that had made him a skilled fighter pilot. He'd been as toasted as anybody the night before, but he'd kept this Sunday evening appointment to create the letter. "Just use *Respectfully yours.* Sets the tone we're goin' for."

"Sounds old-fashioned."

"Nothin' wrong with that."

"If you say so." He scribbled the words.

"Now sign it and we're finished with that part."

"Thank God." He put his signature on the letter. Since he didn't have Badger's iron constitution, he could use some sleep. "Now we can—"

"I hate to tell you, good buddy, but you just signed your name right there."

Damn it. Sure enough, he'd automatically scribbled *Aaron Donahue.* Heaving a sigh, he reached for a blank piece of paper.

"Patience, grasshopper."

Aaron looked up and caught Badger grinning at him. "Not funny."

"Is too. Everythin' about this caper is hilarious." He paused. "You need to stay loose."

"Now you tell me."

"It's just a little play-actin', like when we dressed in drag for the squadron talent show that time."

"But we weren't trying to fool anybody with those wigs and makeup. Convincing Caitlin I'm someone else is gonna be damn near impossible."

"Me givin' her a letter from my old buddy Raven will be a good start."

"And that's the other thing. I'm not Raven anymore. That was in my other life. I haven't used that name since I was discharged. Ryker doesn't answer to Cowboy, either, except when he's with us."

"Every boy and man in Eagles Nest answers to *cowboy.* I wager this town has the highest percentage of cowboys in the—"

"Nevertheless, Ryker and I didn't hang onto our call signs like you did."

"'Cause y'all didn't get saddled with Thaddeus Livingston Calhoun the Third. And I can't help pointin' out that if you'd stuck with yours, you wouldn't be in this pickle."

"Yeah, but I didn't."

"Which is the reason we're goin' to deploy it now. I doubt Caitlin's ever heard us call you Raven. She'll think she's talkin' to a whole different person."

"That letter sure makes me sound like somebody else. I don't recognize that guy."

"Because you're not used to thinkin' of yourself as a hero."

"I'm not—"

"Wounded in action and decorated for valor. Doesn't get much more heroic unless you'd made the ultimate sacrifice. I'm personally delighted that you didn't."

"But I'm not used to talking about any of this."

"You're not talkin' about it. That's the beauty of a letter. That's how an admirer who's hesitant to lay his cards on the table in person handles this kind of situation."

"I'm only hesitant because I've got the same name as her scumbag ex."

"Exactly, and we're goin' to fix that unfortunate situation by presenting her with a genuine war hero she won't be able to resist. I get that you didn't want to put in that you were awarded a medal, but I plan to tell her."

"Please don't."

"Do you want to impress this woman or not?"

He sighed. "Yes, but—"

"Then go with the narrative. It's all true. Shot down behind enemy lines, fought off the enemy and escaped despite a broken leg."

"Only because of Ryker. I told him to leave me."

"Yes, and he's a legend in his own time, but we're focusin' on—"

"We're still not telling him?"

Badger shook his head. "Can't afford to. I'll have my hands full not tellin' Hayley. Which reminds me, we need code words."

"For what?"

"We can't talk about this on the phone if Hayley's around. Or Ryker. Or anybody, come to think of it. You can text me a code word if all's well or a different one if it's effed up. Use *Mach 3* if things are good and *tailspin* if you're scrappin' the mission."

"Okay, but I don't see how you can keep this from Hayley. Or how we'll keep Ryker from finding out. We should tell them."

"Can't. The more who know, the more likely we'll have a leak. Hayley's not a problem. Believe it or not, we go days at a time without mentionin' you."

"Yeah, okay, but we see Ryker all the time. He—"

"I don't want to burden him with a secret he can't tell April. And there's the chance he'll try to talk us out of it."

"Aha! There's the real reason you don't want to tell him."

"Because I've had experience with Cowboy in that regard. When I pretended to be Hayley's fiancée Christmas before last, he was *not* happy that I was foolin' her parents. He told me not to." He spread his hands. "See how wrong he was?"

"Yeah, but this is different."

"Not really. Strictly speakin', I was much less truthful durin' that episode than you'll be durin' this one. You're a *genuine* hero."

Aaron smiled at the way his Southern buddy dragged out the word *genuine.* "Compared to Ryker, I'm not—"

"Don't tell me that you didn't go through hell durin' all those operations on your leg because I know better. That's hero stuff right there."

"So it wasn't a picnic, but—"

"Let's not forget the nightmares."

He shrugged. "Most returning vets have 'em. Nothing unique about that."

"And the freak sandstorm that scratched the corneas in both eyes didn't help, either. They're still sensitive."

"Not *that* sensitive. I was cleared to fly."

"With tinted goggles. Anyway, we have to exaggerate that bit so you can keep the lights low and your ball cap on."

"Badger, this isn't gonna work. She's sharp. She'll figure it out in two minutes."

"You're discountin' the sales job I'll do prior to her showin' up at your house. Southerners are natural storytellers. And charmin' on top of it."

Aaron rolled his eyes.

"If I do my job and turn you into a romantic hero, she'll want to believe. She won't be lookin' for reasons to doubt the setup. A couple of heartfelt conversations in your dimly lit livin' room and she'll start likin' you more'n a bear likes a honeycomb."

"If it gets that far, and I'm not convinced it will, she'll start liking Raven, Aaron's new roommate. How will she take it when she finds out it's been me all along?"

"She might be discombobulated at first, but by then you'll have your foot in the door. She'll realize you two get along like grits and gravy."

"I hope you're right." He scrubbed a hand over his face. "Damn it, why does her ex have to have my exact name, first *and* last?"

"I reckon his momma liked the sound of it, just like yours did."

"Guess so."

"Look at it this way. What have you got to lose?"

"My dignity."

"Tell that to someone who hasn't seen water balloons fallin' out of your dress."

New York Times bestselling author Vicki Lewis Thompson's love affair with cowboys started with the Lone Ranger, continued through Maverick, and took a turn south of the border with Zorro. She views cowboys as the Western version of knights in shining armor, rugged men who value honor, honesty and hard work. Fortunately for her, she lives in the Arizona desert, where broad-shouldered, lean-hipped cowboys abound. Blessed with such an abundance of inspiration, she only hopes that she can do them justice.

For more information about this prolific author, visit her website and sign up for her newsletter. She loves connecting with readers.

VickiLewisThompson.com